I0581563

RUNIE

By: Roland Pierce

Published by:

Zuminstudios

RUNTE
By: Roland Pierce
Copyright 2022
All Rights Reserved.
ISBN: 978-1-7771793-4-2
Cover Art by: Viper Noir (@spectrum_viper)
This is a work of fiction. Any resemblance to people, living or dead are purely coincidental.
Published by: ZuminStudios
www.dei-ex-machina.com
10 9 8 7 6 5 4 3 2 1

Part One

Ruiner

Chapter 1

1

What do I want? You know, really want?
I can't think anymore. All I know is that I have
a longing to go home. What is home? What
exactly defines it for me? I never really had a
home. A place where I felt safe, or loved. Only
when I was really young did I have such fond
memories of a place. And now, I'm not sure. I
was never really sure.

What else can I do? Just stay here lost in
my thoughts of a past life that still gnaws at my
soul. Something I can't abandon or make sense
of in any real way.

However, I do remember the first time I
felt joy. It was when I was young with my

Nanny, Histara. I just called her "Nana" for short. Even though I was young I had no contact with my parents at all. I kind of knew of them, but really, they were nothing more than a blurred-out shape, a shadow that lurked in the darkness just beyond my vision.

Nana was my life and she was in actuality the only person who probably ever cared about me. She took care of me until I was 7, After that, my father finally came to get me. It was traumatizing and confusing.

I remember crying so much it felt like my head would burst. I also remember getting hit more than I ever been up to that point in my life. Nana never hit me before, she never laid a finger on me. However, my father was a different story. He acted like a beast, and never showed any kindness or appreciation for anything I was.

"You were supposed to prepare her for me!" He screamed as I hid behind Nana's dress.

"I-I'm sorry My Lord, I did my best-!" she said bowing and squeezing my hand tight. I looked at them both, large-eyed and confused. Who was this strange man who just popped up in my life out of nowhere? Why was he yelling at us?

"Look at this! Just look at her cowering like some kind of frightened little animal! You call this your best? *Your best?* You should be ashamed!" He hit her so hard that it sent her flying to the floor, I went beside her crying as he grabbed me so hard I felt as if my arm was going to be pulled out from my body I was screaming in confusion.

"Quiet you little brat!" he said, hauling me above his shoulder.

"You'd better pray on your days, Histara! When I come back for you, you'll be begging me for a quick death!"

That was the last time I saw her. He took me into the main house. It was a stuffy place, void of any bright colour, or maybe it felt grey. All the light was drained from here. I could barely see through my tears, but I remember the smell of dust and the faded sunlight.

There the maids cut my hair short like a boy's and prepared me to go into uniform.

"From now on you're a solider!" my father said, "So you'd better fucking act like it! If I see one more fucking tear come out of your eye, I'll gouge it out with a spoon!"

I didn't know what he meant, however, but his tone was so fierce and scary my knees shake from just the sound of him. I wanted to say I wet my pants, but nothing came out. Nothing but a long delay in my memory until I saw the man my father called the "Minister of Education."

He was a whale of a man, white and pale like a massive, bleached blob of gooey dough. I had rarely seen so many strange people when I was with my Nana.

He had this queer smell around him, the smell of cologne, something that I would come to associate with fear and angst in my future encounters.

"So," he said, with a strange kind of tiny voice, "This is your daughter, eh? I guess she could pass for a boy if you sent her to school. At least until she's 12, maybe 13. By then though she should be in boot camp."

"What do you think? Surgical alteration?" My father said.

"Mmmm, no. Physical alteration of any permanent kind is forbidden in the *Concordat of Tsade*-- I know that and you should know that too. If you go ahead, the other families will go after you."

"Damnit.." he hissed, then looked at me with scorn, I looked back at the ground trying not to meet his gaze.

"See! She's just like a tiny little mouse!" he moved and grabbed me by the chin, "Look at me, LOOK AT ME!"

I winced and stared at my father, it was like staring at the sun, I wanted to look away.

"She's a little pussy shit! She can't even look at her father's face. She's not fit to be any kind soldier!" my father said.

"Don't be too hard on her, she is a child after all. I'm sure we can shape her into someone who can be of use in some fashion or another." The Minister said, looking at me and smiling. It was an odd creepy smile, but it was the first smile I seen since I was torn away from my nanny.

"When do we start?" my father asked letting go of my face finally.

"We'll start in the next school year. Allow me to make preparations."

"What? That's in the end of September-- that's four months away!"

"It's standard for people her age." he said, then looked at me again patting my head. "If we go too fast people could get suspicious."

I didn't do or say anything. I couldn't, the moment I did he'd hit me again I'm sure of it.

2

The next couple of weeks were physical and emotional torture. I felt so intimidated and afraid of everything, feeding chickens and cows, cleaning up after animals. The days were from sunrise and sometimes beyond into the night. Even then I was never allowed in the house with the rest of them. They didn't seem to really want to see me around. I spent most of my nights in the barn, hiding in the hay and trying to get warm, I must've not bathed for months after that, but I didn't really care about any of that I never felt so lonely as I did back then. Usually, I found myself crying all day and all night, and then when morning came it started all over again.

I had an idea something was coming, this strange obscure view that I couldn't or wasn't allowed to see. I had no idea or concept as to what "school" was-- all I knew was that whatever was coming must be far worse than what I was going through.

One day while I was working, and I got a massive splinter in my hand.. I went to the help crying unable to tell them what went wrong because I was so upset, so instead I showed them. The maid looked frightened suddenly, so frighten she was shaking.

"You must be more careful!" she as she said removed the splinter, "If something were to happen to you like that we'd all get punished! Not just you!" She ushered me back outside. I was wondering why she would get punished, but as soon as my father saw me coming back from the maid's house, he questioned me right away.

I didn't know what to say, I was just gibbering nonsense.

"I- I- I- hurt-"

"You-you-you what?" he said mocking, almost childish way. "Get back to work, you little bitch!" he smacking me on the bottom pushing me forward. I had to suck back my tears at least until I got back to the barn.

Every day felt like it was getting longer and hotter, I felt like I was starting to lose my mind. It was the middle of the day and must've been 30 C and I was still in the barn cleaning up after the animals. All I wanted was a glass of water but I couldn't- then I noticed these faucets outside with buckets around them. They were suppose to be used for cows but, I managed to sneak in and turn it on under my head. It felt like heaven, but I had to be careful. I had to ensure that nobody saw what I was doing, and I felt as it that it was safe enough.

I want to be clear before I go ahead, that screwing up for me wasn't something that should happen ever. When I did do a half ass job or did something I shouldn't have without permission and was found out, punishment was brutal. Nothing short of a caning would be what I would get and sometimes I was so sore after, that I couldn't even move--it felt like someone took a hot iron to my back.

Although punishment came from my father, I didn't know if I had any other members of my family. I had never met my mother, nor did I know if I had any brothers or sisters--but to an extent I didn't really want to know, either. If they were anything like my father I wanted to stay clear from them.

That night I was beaten for not doing a

good enough job on the pig stall I started up at the cool night into the moon, my fingers, painfully swollen from the work I did previously, still and I wondered where my Nana was and why she wasn't coming to get me. I wondered what I did to deserve any of this, and if this would ever end. And in a way, I thought I could feel something stare back at me... and I didn't know what it was but it felt like a sadness which could not be explained into words or being, and with that I teared up and cried again and didn't know what else I could do, but cry and go back to sleep.

The next day I wasn't sure what was going on, the maids came in and woke me up, changed my clothes then washed me off so vicariously I thought my skin was going to peel off. They did my hair and managed to make it look somewhat feminine. At first I didn't know what was going on at all, it was strange because it felt as if I was getting ready for something- but why dress me up like this? Something this fancy?

"Now be good! For all of our sakes, please be good!" The maids said as they lead me inside the house, I hadn't been inside for a while but it still had this dusty, musty kinda of smell. Like that which haven't been cleaned in a while. The walls looked like a yellowish, and the paintings hanging from the walls looked strange and dark, like hidden shadows within the panels of those frames.

The maids stood with me, as suddenly this strange kind of woman came down the stairs. She was wearing a big long dress, but at the same time she looked extremely pale, her eyes looked like the same colour as mine, an ice blue colour, and she had long black hair. Hair that looked almost like a spider's web with the way in just drifted off her dress.

There was another maid holding her dress behind her and as she finally got to the bottom of the stairs, she grabbed my chin with her long sleek fingers and made me face her in a similar way my father did on an earlier date.

"Hm, So you're Runie are you?" she

said looking at me. I tried to nod but couldn't.

"Yes." I said quietly.

"Hm. I don't see it." she said to the maids around her. They were silent.

The maid stood in silence and said nothing. I looked up confused, unsure what to do or say.

"If you want to be my daughter you're going to have to impress me. Fortunately for you your father has some ideas though I honestly can't imagine what they are. But, honestly, if it was up to me you'd be toss out in the garbage the moment you were born. Instead of a son god cursed me with you, a little demon child! You're nothing but evil! *EVIL!!*"

I couldn't believe it, after all of this, she just came to me to say that? To believe a creature like this was my mother.. so cold, so unfeeling. It was like I was some kind of insect she slapped on her arm.

She turned around to leave and I stepped forward looking at her,

"Where's my Nana?" I asked her,

defiantly.

"How dare you speak to me in that tone you little imp." She hissed, she balled her hands into fists, her glare was almost like a stabbing knife into me. For a moment I thought she wasn't going to hit me, but then stopped as if reconsidering and stepped backward.

"You want to know where your precious 'Nana' is? She's probably dead at the bottom of a thresher. Your father sent her off the a prison camp not long ago because of the disappointment you have become."

I looked up with her in disbelief my mouth gaping open in horror.

"You're *lying*!" I yelled at her.

"Ha! Why would I waste my energy lying to you? You're not worth the time. I mean look at you- you're not woman or man, you're some kind of disgusting half-ling thing that was spat out from my womb! I regretted it ever since!"

"You aren't my mother!" I said glaring at her from my tears.

She dashed toward and slapped me.

"You... take... this... little TWAT out of my HOUSE!" she commanded to the maid. They didn't hesitate and almost dragged me out inside..

Once I was back into the maid's quarters they didn't spend any time taking me out of my dress almost carefully as if I would stain it or something and slapped on the work clothing I was given before tossing me outside like some kind of reject. Then I saw my father my heart sank.. he was strolling up to me with a smirk on his face. I wasn't sure what his reaction was going to be but it felt like it was going to be bad.

"You little snot.." he said and grabbed me by my hair lifting me up, "Still got a bit of spirit in you do you? Well we'll see about that.."

He picked me up and almost threw me into the pig pen- I skidded and looked down as he shoved my face deep into the muck surrounding it.

"Make no mistake, I think it was kind of

funny the way you were able to chew out your mother, but you're not so tough against me are you?" He said pulling my face out of the muck before shoving me back in it, then took me and tossed me back into the barn.

"Don't you dare wash that shit off, I want you to to know what you are, you are shit. And until I tell you otherwise you will always remain shit, got it you little bitch?"

I didn't say anything and just stared at the ground shaking- being unable to say or do anything once again from fear as to what may happen next.

"Remember," my father said holding up his finger to me, "shit only begets shit. And that's what you are..."

All I could do was curl up and cry. You know what? He was right. I was shit. I was worthless. My beloved Nana was probably sent to god knows where and here was I, just curled up into a little ball crying my heart out.

.

The day I got to school I wasn't sure what was going on, but it felt like relief to get away from my family and my father. I still blamed myself though, and it didn't seem like I could get away from that blame. The only person I loved was gone and I would never see her again. However, I didn't see him either, the maids cleaned me up once again and put on my uniform, then I was given my suitcase.

This was the day for "school", I wasn't sure what school was, exactly, only that it was suppose to change me in some way. That it was suppose to make me turn out to be a better "soldier" (whatever that was, my vocabulary wasn't that big at the time), and when I got there with the other children, it looked to be all boys. But none of them really said anything or looked at me. We all kind of looked the same, I was a little taller than the others which made me worried I was going to stick out a bit.

Suddenly an officer came up to me

quickly, looking nervous and put this gold star on my chest. "There we go! Can't go anywhere without this can you??" I looked at the star, it had strange writing on it I didn't understand.

"That's for you. It shows you're from finer stock!" The officer said, "Nobody can touch you with that badge- not the other students, even some of the teachers. Those who don't have this badge at least anyway..." he was wearing a similar badge to mine, it looked like a circle though and was gold and also shiny. I looked at the other kids and they all stared at me suddenly like I turned into a strange kind of monster. What was the deal with this...? They looked away though- and all looked extremely nervous.

As we stood there and waiting at attention the teacher came by, he looked down at his students then saw me, looking at the badge. He also had a golden badge as well.

"In case you didn't know, I am going to be your teacher and commanding officer for the rest of the term. During our time here you will respond with "Yes Teacher" when you are called upon do you understand?"

The rest of the children looked and saluted "Yes, Teacher!"

I stared and stood up straight, worried I was going to do something wrong.

"You!" He pointed right at me with his long bony finger and walked up to me, "You've got a problem with me?"

I shook my head quietly and violently hoping for him to forget about me, for them all to disappear at once. That didn't happen though and I was stuck there, stuck in that place.

"Good, then you say 'YES TEACHER!' Understand?!" the teacher said, "Let me hear you say it!"

"Yes teac-"

"LOUDER! SCREAM IT!"

"YES TEACHER!" I screamed, my face red, I was worried my face was going to explode or something.

"Excellent!" he said turning around, "You people do what I say, and we'll have a great school year- Don't, and you will have a very awful school year.."

I looked down trying to control myself from shaking- digging my hands into my pockets, and by the time he was finished speaking I was very close to wetting myself. Didn't happen, so I suppose I was lucky.

When we were ushered inside I was in awe at how beautiful the hall was, it looked like a massive arc of engraving around it with statues in various poses. The floor was gleaming almost like glass and the doors were all polished with the room numbers emblazoned over the top of them.

I was lead through the area and corned off, the students seem to be going towards what looked to be a medical office, I on the other hand, was ushered away by another teacher wearing a golden seal as well and told to walk towards the office.

"You, this way-" he said.

"But I-"

"Never mind about them-"

I nodded, defeated, I seemed to be doomed to be wandering around here with some kind of confused layer over me of things that will never be explained or excepted.

As I went to the office a man was there with a skinny moustache, he looked like a doctor perhaps but seemed all too tired or irritated to possibly be one.

"Is this the student? Runie Oritix?" He said looking at a board before placing it down.

"Y-yes!" I said in a wispy tone.

"Hm.. Do you ascertain that the subject is about to be examined by a medical professional is it your opinion that I proceed in the matter of the Golden Kin?" He asked the other officer.

"Yes. You are permitted."

With that he checked my mouth and teeth, he checked my height and weight and asked if I was in pain or felt pain anywhere.

"No." I said.

He seemed to look over every inch of me and was very quick, at that point he told me to get dressed and I left. I didn't feel any less awkward than I did before, but oddly enough it didn't seem like a true examination, especially in retrospect, in fact it all seemed like a joke. Like I was some kind of animal like a horse or a pig.

Once I was finished they set me back to the living quarters, separated from the other students. It looked like it was kind of weird empty warehouse used for something else totally different. There was a few beds there and some stacked in the back, they also had different dressers and things set up including a foot locker. I was wondering what the point of this was.. I had no idea of how different or why I was being so singled out.. but of course it was obvious. One I was a girl, two I was a member of the golden circle.

The golden circle, or kin circle was a fancy name for the families which actually ran the country, 12 to be exact. One of which I was from and my father was the head of, the others all had their own agendas and their own protocols, but from what I read later on, they all ran the country exactly the same way. They prey and manipulated the weak while the others just drank their blood on the way to the future. It's exhausting to think about, but all the animals that just grow to feed themselves feel like how the way this country is run. And as I got settled in and began to read the so-called "welcome" book they gave me... I felt more and more like I was going down a void I couldn't get out of, or couldn't see the bottom of.

It was totally ignorant of me, everything involving my culture, country, being, everything was totally new nature to me and seemed totally alien. I didn't know anything for the past years of my life and certainly didn't know anything but pain and abuse for the past few months. Reading this booklet they gave me, wasn't just some kind of joke, it was for a test. A test they were going to give tomorrow and I was frightened to know what happens if you failed in a school such as this, especially how my father treated me for simply just

screwing up on things while working on the
farm.

A Great Tapestry

A look at our country's history

*Through the years of out great conception, our
great nation has overcome many different
struggles
from those who would dare oppose us.
The Amalek, those who would stand and
oppose us in any way fashion or form, as those
who would stand against us have become
Amalek and Amalek shall become our enemies.
But none could stand, would stand, will stand
against our great nation as a whole, let those
who dare be cast aside and wiped away from
this earth as designated by Y-h.
The fact that we still stand today after
millennia of being slaves to the past, slaves to*

those who abused us, slaves to our former so called "Fatherland". None can oppose us now. Let the reign of Mesopelagia be complete and those who will help it pave the way to the future be on their blood, and yours!!

I had no idea what any of this was at the beginning, I am still kind of vague on a lot of details.. but as I continued reading things just fell apart from there. I didn't have no idea what this was.. and a lot of the words made zero sense to me. But through the years I managed to make more sense of what it was saying and I didn't like it, I didn't like any of it.

The history

Our great conception was that thousands of years ago far away in the forsaken country of Judah, who would dare use us as slaves and those who would dare would be smited and be

destroyed. Luckily for us, and unluckily for them, the kingdom of Israel also sent their own settlers towards this
great new land and the new land thrives underneath them. Years and years passed, as time came along our Great forefathers took the greatest of men and the greatest of women and combined them into a new sect, the sect of our leaders and those who would paint the new way towards our future.

As the years passed, the Judahs thought of us as nothing more than slaves, but once we became the leaders of our own tribes we suddenly started to begin new ideas, new inventions, new ways to live that have never been fathomed before, and thus a new Jewish colony was formed, the kingdom of Mesopelagia. The true
land of the Jews, the true race anointed by God.
God had allowed us to finally use his own name

and not in vain as the pathetic races before it thought to but we were able to command the name of God, that is our gift. Our gift is freedom and the freedom to finally command the name of the Lord in respect.

Now with our two kingdoms combined, Judah and Israel, we finally launched all out war on the new Amaleks which plagued us, the Judahs and the Israelites. The fake race that was once chosen by the lord now favoured us and we done away with them with the force that the Lord would be proud of. After the war which occurred sometime ago we were able to smite them to their final resting place, across the globe in their pathetic desert and with loneliness as we reign supreme on the land, the seas and the continent of this wondrous new land. The land of Mesopelagia.

Who were... the jews? What? I wasn't sure if any of this made sense. Nobody told me anything. I had no idea or belief in any of

this. The things they were telling me were going right over my tiny little head. Right now all I wanted to to was sleep or get away. Or do something else, anything else besides read this book over. It just felt like they were talking and babbling endlessly for no apparent reason.
If I had been older, I'd say they were committing self-fellatio .

Although I was curious I wasn't sure if I should believe what was being said regardless I continued onward.

The future

We are blessed by the future. We are anointed by God. The meek shall inherit the earth, and we are the meek, the meekest of the meek from thousands of years of slavery, abuse, bloodshed, innovation.
From the years that move forward we will allow those who wish to join us, to join, and those who are not will be the enemies of the

*future and be wiped off the globe. We shall
spread our wings to the seas and beyond, and
soon, the others, the nations of the world, and
you will know the true
power of Mesopelagia and the power it seeks.
The power granted to us by the heavens,
the power which we wield to defend peace
and justice, the power we will enforce on those
who will take advantage of the weak and
enfeebled.
God bless our race, our chosen people,
and God bless Mesopelagia!*

Our Golden Circle

*With the help of our glorious families, we
enable to move the country forward
from the view that only the best should do the
most important work. As a
result, we have ensured those with proper
bloodlines around the nation to
take command and ensure we continue on the
right path of history. If you are a member of the*

*Golden Circle, you have a great responsibility ahead
of you, you must ensure to be an example to all
who will one day be
under your command. If you are not, do not
worry, for you are still play
an important role in our society!*

The Families of the Glorious golden circle

*Memorize these. For these families are future
leaders of the world! With
your respect and acknowledgement, we can
move towards a bright future for
all!*

Ramely
Shultx
Commarian
Tumara
Xonarx
Efron
Ortix

Ackerman
Goldberg
Hoffman
Pereira
Vingerhuot

The Grey Circle

*If the golden circle was the brains the grey
circle is the muscule. Without you
we would not be able to move forward with the
future, the plan. The moment you
are born, you have become one of the most
valuabe people on earth. The Chosen
Ones, the destiny! Value this state, for it will
ensure that you will have your
place in history.*

Peasants

*These are the filter class. Although they may
never serve, they are important to
our lively hoods as well. For they help do the*

*jobs we cannot. They help maintain
the lives of such tiny medial work which are
important to us none the less. Keep
this in mind, and treat them with respect.*

You

*Without you, we are nothing. We cannot help
but move forward without your help. Your
blood,
your tears, your sweat, it will all feed into
our great nation and when you join us, you
become the nation. You become something
greater than yourself. You will become
the sword and the shield, the meekest of the
meek. The innovator and the excavator.
Chosen by God.
You will help enable us to protect against
the Amaleks. The destroyers. The
terrorists that would dare come and defile
this land which rightfully belongs to us
as anointed by God!*

Our national Anthem

O nation of the Lord
O nation of the sword
those who would oppose us
would be
severed eternally

Meekest of the meek
Weakest of the weak
we look upon this land
which have been given to us by hand
and thus the world is ours
thus world is yours
With weapons to be
granted and blessed by the divine
the sights and smells
the light will shine

Sea to sea
Ground to sky

Am I really free? I wish I knew for sure, regardless my mind really couldn't interrupt the words in the book very well. Everything seemed to be coming at me at once and hard. My head was starting to hurt. I wished that I was somewhere else anywhere else, and the guilt and shame of me, somehow deserving this was ringing in my brain. The only thing I could do now was read these small books and hope to god that I was able to remember it.

The meekest of the meek, the weakest of the weak? Give me a break. Whoever wrote this must've been totally deluding themselves. As far as I was concerned, it was all lies. But I suppose anyone with half a brain could see something so blatantly wrong. Then again, maybe not. I could see how the kids in my class would think how "cool" this was, but to me, it was all just nonsense. That's what it felt like, this situation, me, everything, all nonsense.

Chapter 2

1

The next day they made us take a test, it actually wasn't too hard even though I my ability to read was lacking. There were those who didn't past, and some of the students seemed to be in pain physically for some reason, though from what, I had no idea. Probably some kind of weird disciplinary act. Regardless they announced the marks in front of the class, and I was a bit embarrassed.

The teacher was actually helpful, but seemed to be annoyed with everything. Regardless though, he seemed to be impressed with me. He decided though that I may need more extra attention and this felt odd. It was the only time I wasn't disciplined for being bad. If my father was there I'm sure I'd get up getting whipped every time I screwed up.

I didn't mind school, however, the other students seemed to avoid me like the plague. They didn't want anything to do with me, and when lunch came around I was forced to sit alone.

I was actually kind of smart in some things, but in other things I was really stupid. Really stupid. I couldn't help but screw up math. Math was my worse subject, I could barely add 2 and 2 together to get any meaningful answers.

Languages was somewhat easier because I loved to read- and I liked writing, but my teacher told me my writing was horrible and almost illegible. I still continued to write and write, and though it was difficult at first I started to enjoy it.

The books and things they gave us to read though were somewhat dry and uninteresting. They were mostly about the nation's history and things that involved the military.

If Jeb had 4 bullets and fired 3, how many bullets would he have left. Things like this. When it came to "break time" most people spent it studying or practising. Not too many children went out to play and those who did seemed to be doing some kind of military games and things like that, practising marching, doing physical exercises like push ups and things like this and that. It didn't really dawn on me, the stark reality of the situation until they started combat training. Simple target shooting was enough for us, and I couldn't believe how unimaginably heavy the gun felt, and it felt heavier still when it was stocked with bullets. I didn't seem to be the only one who had problems either. A lot of the other students seemed to be having issues with holding their weapons as well.

"As you know, a soldier is nothing without their weapon! So from today on, you will get to know it, you will sleep with it, it will be your best friend! Understand?"

"Yes teacher!" everyone shouted.

The first time I took it apart I cut myself up kind of bad and I was in shock with the blood that gushed up over everything.

"Would you look at this mess?!" The teacher hissed and took the gun away, throwing it on the ground.

"You go see the doctor right now damnit! Before you bleed all over your uniform!"

I looked down at my hands and my eyes were full of tears as I went to the doctor's office. There the doctor glanced at me as if he was annoyed and looked at my hands.

"Oh, this is nothing." he said, and sighed grabbing them and washing them roughly in the sink before slapping on some bandages. I still got the odd feeling from him, this strange kind of feeling that I should probably get out of there as soon as possible but I didn't know what it was, not until sometime later.

When I returned the teacher looked pale, like he saw a ghost or something, and that's when I realized why, my father was there and he did not look very pleased.

He sighed and looked at teacher until he noticed me, then picked me up so hard I thought he was going to pull my arm out of the socket.

"You said she was doing well, what the hell is this?"

"Sir, she has been excelling at other subjects, it's my opinion that this kind of situation could be easily rectified."

"It is your opinion is it? And you're suppose to be in charge of all these little snots, let's see how they shoot, go ahead, show me what you all learned!"

I was going to look down at the ground but then I thought about what happened before and refused to look down, just staring wide eyed as he shoved the gun into my hand.

"You first-" he said, "*See!* Just to show I don't play favourites, nor do any of the other commanding officers in this army- I am willing to let my own son go first- go ahead, shoot the fucking target."

I didn't even know how to operate this thing yet, let alone shoot anything. I stared and the teacher looked away, he didn't seem to want anything to do with me and I was on my own.

I turned and looked at the target..

"Sir, I haven't taught them how to shoot yet-"

He hit his forehead and growled, his face own turning purple as he sighed, "Well, what the fuck are you waiting for?!" he yelled, then went into the back and sat down grumbling as he showed everyone the basic operation of the gun.

"Is that clear?"

I was still fuzzy on it, but I had an idea of what to do now at least.

"Okay, Runie, you go first."

I gulped hard, and didn't know exactly what to do, line up my shot, check, uhhh--I forgot the rest and started to shake. The only thing I remembered was squeeze don't pull the trigger.. so I squeezed and waited and finally the gun with off and almost hit me in the face. I turned and held my mouth wondering if i broke anything or not.

The teacher looked through at the target and suddenly started to shake. I guess I didn't do a good enough job, because that's when my father looked at us and left. I thought for sure he was going to give me a beating but it didn't seem to be in the cards.

Next day though the teacher was gone, and replaced with someone else. This man still had a different kind of seal on him that was in gold but I got a real bad feeling from him. Like he didn't want to be there are all, like he was forced into this mess and he all gave us this strange ice cold stare.

"STUDENTS! My name is Dejarrger Torlence! I have been assigned to you as your teacher for the remainder of the term." He said walking around.

I was worried, worried that whatever

happened to the old teacher was my fault. It always seemed to be my fault no matter what I did. There was no way to fix it.

"I don't know what your last teacher was teaching you, or how he was teaching you. But I am here to inspire discipline and justice. Those of you may not agree with my methods, and may think I am 'too strict' and too aggressive. However, those under my command and teaching have become the strictest and most disciplined military men in the whole goddamn nation!

"Those of you who do well, will be treated well. And those who don't, will face the rod!" he said and slapped the top of his desk with a large rubber stick that looked black with big knots in it.

"Understand?!" he his voice echoed through out the class room.

"Yes Teacher!" I along with everyone else said so loudly so there was no misunderstanding on what was being told to us.

"Good."

The next days that came upon me were extremely stressful and scary.. each time we made a mistake he would instantly hit us with that rubber rod of ours. On more than one occasion he would hit us several times for failing to get any answers wrong of any kind. It was almost surreal. I was wondering what this could possibly accomplish but I didn't have the guts to say or do anything. I couldn't. What would someone expect? Me to take on someone five times my size.. what would anyone expect from this?

One day my fingers were so swollen that I couldn't even write anymore, the pain from being hit was starting to get to me and I was starting to get a rumbling in my stomach like I was going to be sick. Not to mention the slight twinge in the back of my head. I looked at the clock, just 50 more minutes before class ended.

"Runie!" The teacher finally turned around and pointed that stick right to me. I jumped and my stomach lurched, and I held my hand over my mouth. I'm not sure what he was asking me, something about some kind of obscure reference towards a math question or something like that.

"So, what's the answer then?"

I stood up, dizzy, not able to really get a hold of myself, and when I opened my mouth I wanted to say "I think I'm gonna be sick"- instead vomit just poured out from it on the desk and all over. The students stared and looked freaked out, so did I, I had thrown up all over my uniform and papers and everything in front of me.

I didn't see anything but the mess made on the ground and I felt as if I was going to pass out. He grabbed me and picked me up, I was totally ignoring him- but I remember what he said to me.

"What are you doing?!" He spat, "You think this is funny?! Now lick it up!" he said, and shoved my face to the floor. I didn't do anything, I couldn't- I just felt the odd numbness and the feeling of leaving my body somewhere. I did feel when he shoved my face once again to the floor so hard I could barely breath but after that everything was a blur and I found myself back at the doctor's office- one my eyes was swelled shut and I had a splitting headache but I wasn't ill anymore. It felt strangely calm and white, almost beautiful. I knew this wasn't a feeling that was going to last though. As soon as the doctor comes back he's going to yell at me, or my father was going to come in and finish the job they started. But nobody came in, at all, for 20 minutes. How long was I left alone in here..? I didn't know. I didn't even know what time it was- but everything just kinda felt melted together.

I'm not sure the time that passed, I figured it was about half an hour when the doctor finally slipped back in. He seemed to have this odd little devilish look on his face that I didn't like.

"So, how are you feeling now? Are you sleepy.." he said, flashing a light into my eyes.

"No." I said, wondering if he was going

to do anything else.

"Well, it doesn't look like you're suffering from any kind of concussion." he said and smiled, maybe he was trying to become friends with me or something. But it was just the fact he was looking at me strangely. I'm not sure. I never had anyone to be friends with before, and I only been close to my Nana so I was oddly paranoid around him. But I didn't feel like I wanted to be in this room much longer.

"I've given you these tablets.." he finally said, "if you experience any kind of pain but they will make you a bit drowsy. I informed your instructor though of this so he will keep this mind while doing so. I gave you one by injection as soon as you came in.."

I stared and started to get up, only to find I was wearing some kind of gown underneath. "W-what happened to my clothing?"

"Oh, we took them off," he said and cleared his throat, "But we got you a new outfit, just take some time to get dressed and we you can go back to your quarters."

I nodded, waiting for him to leave but he didn't. So I ended up getting dressed and then left,
feeling unnerved.

2

When I got back, the pain was returning again. Not from my head but to my hands. They were beaten, and bent so severely I couldn't even hold a book. I'm don't believe they were broken, but it was certainly distracting. I had some hard time opening the bottle as well, it felt like this was a weird kind of sadistic game. For some reason I couldn't get a grip, but I finally managed to get it open when I put it under my shirt and turned it. Some of them fell on the floor, but I managed to gather them up.

It seemed like he wasn't too concerned about me overdosing, or doing anything of that nature. I was young and just giving this stuff to a 7 year old, hoping she won't take the whole bottle felt needlessly risky.

I tried to read the bottle: "Take as needed. 1 pill every 8 hours or as advised." I'm not sure what "advised" meant, but I understood everything else and took one with some water from the rusted out sink in the hangar. And, I tell you, once it hit me it hit me hard. I felt extremely tired and just stared at the ceiling. All the pain was gone, but I felt unable to really do much but stare, everything felt.. odd to me. Like I couldn't move my body.

I stared, then notice something rustling around in the dark. I thought for sure I was imagining it, it felt like the shadows were starting to move on their own. And as I looked, the shadows rippled through across the wall- stretching up and over the ceiling and downward. Suddenly little tiny specks of what looked like light was shining through them. But they weren't any kind of light I have ever seen before, they seemed oddly.. rainbow-ish in colour. As soon as I looked away, the rays looked like this beautiful colourful rake of some sort. But the shadow just moved and soon the eyes turned and started to look more realistic, weirdly reddish and purple in colour.

It looked at me and the look itself started to make me feel panic. Like it was trying to influence me, or just scare me into something by simply just looking at me. I could feel this odd kind of static coming off it, the weirdly darkness slowly started to take over the whole hangar, and now the only source of light remaining was the lamp over my bed. Of course along with the tiny red specs of light staring down at me, staring at me as if to try to frighten me somehow and it was working. It didn't say anything to me, and it didn't half to.

As I drifted off I felt as if the light was getting weaker and weaker, but the static sounds from this strange force was moving away from me at fantastic speed.

I woke up later at around 3am. It felt like it was forever ago and I felt stark awake. These pills were extremely powerful.. and I felt that this could be a little dangerous. I was a bit afraid that was able to sleep through so easily.

I tried to get up and tidy up a bit later, and when it was time to leave for school I took a few of those pills with me, keeping the rest of them in my dresser underneath my clothing and such. I was pretty sure nobody ever checked there and I was starting to wonder what my father might think if I actually had them.

The teacher was still there once I returned and I saw he didn't seem to actually get into any trouble. But maybe he did. My desk was cleaned and nobody said anything to me. It was like it never happened. Not only that he never called on me the whole day, I was starting to question maybe if I existed at all.

As soon as class was done I was able to get everything back, my eye was a lot better than before as well. I was lucky that I didn't get hit at all by him that time, so maybe he did get told to not over do it.

Before we left the teacher added. "Now, come the next few weeks we will begin physical training. So I want to ensure all of you follow the diets that are given to you- and DO NOT, eat outside of the expected regime, understand?"

"Yes teacher!" everyone said.

"Good, we will also be introducing skills related to shooting, assembly and disassembly of your weapon, recon, and others. This is what you have been prepared for, and in the coming months we will slowly ramp up this training as we go along."

The homework they gave us was standard stuff, nothing too interesting and I found that I was starting to yearn for some kind of reading content that was. I read the booklet again when I first came here, though it felt that it was somewhat lacking in any creativity I felt that it was better than nothing. I started to read more instructional books and even read ahead in my student math and Yiddish books, and anything else that I could come across. I even started to read the books and labels for empty meal canisters and things left in the hangar.

I didn't take any more of the medication that day, I still felt a bit of pain but I didn't like what I saw when I took it before and tried to shrug it off as I went to sleep I had an extremely odd dream, this dream like I was watching everyone and everything but I didn't have any kind of body. It felt as if I was watching everything at once and flying through space and stars at the same time. I tried to look down I think I saw my home world. I'm not sure, but it looked like it was encircled and on fire.

Fire ranging from all the continents and the dark side had those odd kind of red lights coming from it as before. But I didn't fear them, they were below me, nothing compared to me. I felt as if I knew what they were and what they wanted, and I knew they couldn't hurt me, not now, not ever. But, I was a different being. This sense of loneliness was high suddenly, and as I looked out beyond the stars and time I couldn't help but feel this screaming from beyond. And the one who was screaming was me, inside my own head.

3

The next week was far more gruelling than anything before. They gave us mock equipment and things like guns and made us start marching as soon as class started. Luckily, or maybe unluckily we weren't the only ones out. It was a cloudy and almost dull like day, but the air felt strangely energizing.

After the first part of morning training was over, they had us assemble and disassemble our weapons, over and over again for the next two hours. This time I didn't cut myself, and was able to do it easily. In fact, it felt like it was second nature to me. At the end they started to time us to see how fast we could do it, I did mine in less than 5 minutes, which seemed to cause the teacher to actually praise me.

"Holy shit, cadet! You almost made a school record! You keep this shit up and we will be proud to call you a golden seal!"

"Thank you sir!" I said. I wasn't sure why this was such a good thing.. it was simply taking it apart, I was amazed by the fact that I could do it without hurting myself though.

The afternoon was the worse because it started to rain and they all made us do an insane amount of push-ups with the pack sacks still on. It wasn't just us, it was all the students outside. I was wondering exactly what the point of this was. Were we actually going to be doing this a lot later on? I mean, was there any other point or just to build strength?

I had a hard time with it though, I wasn't able to do the push-ups correctly and was slower than normal but nobody really seemed to pay any mind. People were too focused on their own troubles and situations to bother with me.. little did I know the worse was soon to come.

It had come to my belief that the fact we were going to do target practice made me feel as nervous as before. I wasn't in pain as much either, all my wounds had gone away, but when they took out the men in handcuffs in front of us, this strange curiosity slowly dawned upon me.

What were they doing with those men all chained up and dirty? They looked like criminals of some sort. One looked so beaten his face was nothing more but red swellings, I began to wonder if that man could see anything through that face.

"Alright cadets!" The teacher said, "Today we will be using live targets, it's pretty simple. Just do the same as you did last time, aim, and fire."

He held up one of the rifles that looked similar to the ones we were issued and aimed to a random inmate, shooting him in the shoulder.

The man grunted, but didn't scream as

the blood gushed from his wound. He looked almost like he was biting his tongue to prevent himself from making a sound.

"Alright who's first...? Any volunteers..??"

Some other boys raised their hands and looked rather eager to give it a try. I was wondering what was wrong with them all, it seems like everyone here had gone mad or something. "Go ahead! Show those *drek* who's boss!"

The boy took more than one shot, one buzzed around the man's head, another looked like he just barely hit him on the side of his arm."

"You just skinned him-"

"Let me do it again! I can hit him if I can do it again!" the young boy said.

"You all will get your chance don't worry.."

A number of students started to line up, all except me. I just stared at the man who I was suppose to shoot, not sure what I was suppose to do.”

"Cadet Oritix!" The teacher said coming up towards me, do you have a problem?”

I looked nervously back and fourth holding my rifle down confused.

"I uh-" I fumbled through my words.

"Well what the fuck are you waiting for?! Get in position and take the shot!”

"Well- but.." I looked at the man in front me me, "Is this.. really.. right? I mean-”

"Yes it's right! Of course it's right! It's right because I say so!" he said screaming in my face. "Now assume the position and take the shot!" he said, smacking me on the side of the ear.

My eyes bubbled up in tears, despite the fact I was hit so many times I still couldn't really take being hit. Something just came up deep inside my body, hot and wet and made my insides stir causing me to tear up inside.

"Now take aim and shoot that *behemia*!!" he said and pointed at the man in front of me. The man looked scared and at first didn't seem to actually know where he was, or perhaps what he was seeing. The other shots rang out through the air, another prisoner started to suddenly sob, one was making this awful gargling noise that sounded like a tub draining of water.

"Don't make me get the General here cadet! If your father has to come here and see you acting like a whiny little pussy he'll be far more angry at you than he will be at me!"

I sighed and shook, looking through the site, not sure what to do.. my eyes were so full of tears I didn't even look straight. All I could hear is the teacher screaming at me and the shots from the other guns going off. I gritted my teeth and fired, the shot just went way over his head, splintering the wall behind him.

"You missed!" the teacher said, grabbing me by the hair and shaking me. "You did that on purpose you little shit!!"

"AH! No sir I am not!" I said, almost yelling.

"Then why did you miss him?!"

"I didn't mean to sir, please!" He pulled back on my hair harder and I let out a yell, it was at this point all the shooting stopped and I could fell the stares of the other students burn on my skin.

"Then shoot that faggot and stop acting like a little baby!" the teacher said.

I tried to shoot him again but got distracted. One of the other prisoners started to weep and sob, asking for the guards to kill him.

"Shut up before I cut your fucking dick off, cunt eater!" the teacher said.

I was shaking so much, all this seemed wrong, so wrong- I had to get out of this somewhere or somehow.

"Teacher," I said, "I think I'm gonna be si-"

"Don't you pull that bullshit on me again! You might've done it once but you won't get away with it this time!" He said and pulled my hair again before letting it go suddenly, "I don't care if you shit your fucking pants you're gonna shoot at that man until he is DEAD. D-E-

A-D. Dead, do you understand cadet?"

I nodded furiously, or tried to anyway.

"I want to hear 'YES TEACHER!' Understand?? Now say it!"

"Yes teacher!" I yelled.

I heard the people around me giggle, and others whispering behind me.

"Please.." the older prisoner said, hanging..

The teacher looked up, his face was turning a purple colour. He took out a knife and handed toss it to another soldier."

"Cut that old' cunt's tongue out."

"SIR!" The guard said saluting. Turning around and stared to do what he was told. Well I was pretty sure he did. The blood curdling screams could be heard from that direction. Shortly there after the guard threw some red and bloody flesh on the ground. I looked away.

The teacher growled and shoved my head down, grabbing my head and shoving it down into the ground. "Okay, enough!" He said, I could barely breath as he pulled me back up shoving his large meaty hands against my small fingers he stared and forced me to aim.

"AIM, FIRE!" he said, pulling so hard I could feel the pinch from the flesh of my skin. He fired again and again..

Blood suddenly speckled out from the man's chest and he just stared, with the same expression of horror he hand earlier.

"That's it. Cadet, get your ass out of this class right this minute!! You want to be a pansy so much you can go and sit there and watch how real soldiers behave!"

I sat there, tired and defeated. Not sure what was going to happen next, only imagining my father coming out and beating the shit out of me. It dawned at me at this point how much I hated this place, it's people, my fellow students, all of them. They were all just human garbage. My Nana taught me to respect others, and treat them well. These people weren't like that.. they were all horrible. But maybe that's hot the world really was.. maybe she was the exception and now I was.. I wasn't sure but I started to wonder if there was a way out maybe, somehow.

I sat there not sure how long, maybe half an hour as the students peppered and shot the prisoners full of bullets until they were silent and bloody.

The teacher told me to stay there as they all went back inside. I stared as the other guards came up and shot each of the prisoners in the head. It didn't really occur to me that out of all the horrible things I saw today, this was the most merciful thing that they could do. I was pretty sure they were dead already however.

It was probably another hour until my father showed up. He stared at me silently.

"You're such a disappointment." he said growling, "Maybe I should take you and put you up against that wall and let the others take shots at you."

I looked up at him, petrified. That thought didn't occur to me at all, and like a spark it just came out of me.

"No-no! Don't do that!"

"Oh! You don't like that do you..??" he said, grabbing me by the arm again and tugging throwing me over his shoulder.

"W-why, why are you doing this?!" I said, crying.

"Because you need to realize what it's like to be in this army!" he said, pushing me against the wall. "You either are the predator or the prey!"

He stepped back grinning..

"Don't move too much, or maybe you should run, because if you do you won't get shot!"

I looked up at him with my eyes wide and crazed, not sure what I should do. Should I run? Or just stay where I was.. I didn't know.. I just decided to get down and huddle in a ball hoping he was joking. Hoping this was all just a dream, and that it will end as soon as he pulls that trigger and shoots me.

"Stop acting like a goddamn baby!" he yelled, and pulled the trigger, the gun firing, I could hear the bull whiz by me. He pulled it again, and again, until there was wood and splinters popping and flying all around my head. I didn't move, I thought for certain I was shot and was going to bleed to death. All I could do was just huddle there, and after it was done the only thing I could hear was my father, laughing.

"Oh boy.." he said, rubbing his face, "I tell you, I needed that! I needed that so bad.." he said, and emptied the gun from it's shells. "Get up and go back to your quarters.." he said, still trying to hold back his laughter.

I didn't look up, I couldn't. I couldn't even see walk straight. My legs all felt like rubber and powerless, like they were going to give out on me at any moment. I was worried he was behind me, still when I got into the hall- still when I made my way outside to the hangars outside, and when I finally got in and closed it behind me I was so glad, so glad I could just collapse and cry myself into silence.

As the weeks passed by I got use to the noise. I got use to the screams and sobbing and I got use to using my gun. I wasn't any good at it though, when there weren't live targets I shot I wasn't hitting those very well either. It turned out I was a shitty shot, among other things I started to lag behind everything else. It's like something extremely horrible happened to me and all of the spirit in my body was drained. Hm, I wonder what that could've been?

I soon became more and more aware I couldn't just defy everything they wanted me to do. I was dragged into this life, my past life was something that could never return (at least at this point anyway), so I tried to continue on and do what was expected of me. I managed to get away with a lot of things but it dawned on me that after my father nearly killed me. Not that he might actually do it- I'm not sure what was going through his head most of the time. Sometimes I wonder why he just didn't give up on me, why was he putting so much effort in making sure I would become a solider? What was the point? I didn't know. I couldn't think of anything that would allow him to continue to bother with me. But as the weeks and months rolled away it came to me that he maybe he did care for me- maybe this was his sick and twisted way of telling me he had faith in me in some way. The thoughts began to gnaw and me, and I was starting to wonder if I shouldn't perhaps try to look at the matter through his point of view- through other's point of view. That maybe what I was witnessing was somehow really my fault. I sort of resigned myself to this thinking. Maybe this is just his way of telling me he loved me, I mean no parent would totally hate their child would it? Should I be proud that I am getting through this, should I be continue on and just do what they ask of me or fear of getting slapped or worse..? I didn't know, all these thoughts were swirling around my head and I was unable to think clearly. From then on I went on autopilot.

Anything they asked, I tried my best to do, and if I couldn't do it I just risked waiting for the slap on the head or where ever it was coming from.

I tried my best to past the tests, the whole academics were easy, I was getting better and better at reading, and my writing was a lot better too, but my math still sucked. They didn't seem to be as worried about that though. What they were worried about was me being able to crawl through the muck and the blood. They cut up pigs and hung them upside down to make us do this, and the smell and the dirt of it, sometimes I wanted just to cry underneath it and not more forward and I wasn't the only one. Lots of the other children did the same thing. I didn't, I was tired of being beaten and yelled at. I just had to keep going on, just keep going on and ignore it and it will get better then none of this will matter anymore. The rain, and the exhaustion, the fact that sometimes all of my body hurt from the exercise.. every once and a while I would take those pills when I couldn't sleep, but I never seen that black thing again.. well not from the pills at least.

When it came to me a lot of people didn't mention a lot of things I did ever again. I was almost like a ghost, a figment of people's imagination and soon I would come to realize how right I was about that.

I tried to stay behind and hide in the shadows when it came to things, but sometimes it seemed that my teacher had other plans. He would call on me every once and a while to repeat equations and mantras from the books they gave us.

I read every one, not out of some semblance of loyalty but mostly curiosity. I asked for more once and he told me I should keep my mind more on my studies than reading pointless "shit" as he said. My imagination though could not have me satisfied by some most propaganda lies though and I tried to find something to read anywhere I could. I went to the library there, which I was told had vast numbers of books, but was told by the person in charge that no book could be taken out without permission from their teacher or a "high power".

I went back defeated.. and simply went back to my studies, as repugnant as some of them were it did help me pass the time and ease the pain of actually going through the tests and everything else.

The months passed and soon we were at the end of the year. And as the year ended, I couldn't help but feel lighter. At least so I thought anyway.. until the last day came.

When we all came into class that last day, all the desks were gone and moved near the windows. On the floors where what looked to be some kind of cloth with plastic laid out all over the room. We were all confused as to what was going on.

Above there were what looked to be ropes, and pulleys, I never realized those were there before but, it was simply kind of dark above in this place. It was a crumbly little wooden room of course, and as the guard came in he almost slammed down the chair in the middle of the room, giving us a strange look before leaving.

Then shortly after our teacher entered, "Well cadets it looks like we have a little 'treat' for you on this last day of study before the summer. After this you will be given your final papers indicating whether you pass or fail. I tell you, this is part of your final grade. How you perform today will be taken into account whether you pass, or fail." He overlooked the rest of us with a steely stare.

"This is a real piece of shit, a genuine *fagala*. But if you do as I instruct, when and ONLY then.. you will be rewarded." He looked back at the other guards who seemed to be, odd. They looked like they were staring through something that wasn't there. Then they went back outside for a moment, where a number of other officers came in dragging a man behind them. He looked beaten and smelled of some kind of rotten flesh. His face was puffed up and it looked like he was a prisoner for some time.

"Cadets, this is Stephen Cortman. Once holding the rank of Lieutenant and a grey ghost, he pissed that all away for some kind of pitiful excuse for a bride. He's a grey-ghost like the lot of you, and as a result he's tainted that rank. *TAINTED IT!*" he said.. taking off his gloves.

"You're the one w-who.. who is tainted.." Cortman began, but the teacher continued.

"NOT only was he excepting bribes from foreign agencies against our great nation, but he also had several surprising texts which were banned from any kind of possession or distribution. Isn't that right, Stephen?"

"Fuck you asshole!" he managed to say through busted lips.

"AH! Watch your language around the children would you. Unlike you, they will make a great contribution to our nation some day."

"Not if they knew the truth they wouldn't-"

The teacher's hand was quick as a lightning flash and slapped him across the mouth hard. "See, children, people like this, they'll tell lies, they will say anything at the end to prove their point is wrong when the final time comes.."

I looked nervously, wondering what was going to happen, were they going to kill him here? Or make us do something? Maybe we were suppose to see what it was like to witness an interrogation..

"But, unlike you, I will show... some kind of common sense." the teacher said, "Now, think very carefully of what you say next.. I will give you a chance to save your soul and the souls of your wife and child.."

"They're already dead..." Cortman said.

"Oh no! Not yet.. they're not dead yet. But they will be soon!"

"I seen you kill them!!" He spat at the teacher.

"Oh them, they were just scofflaws of something else.. Nothing really of any important note.. but I will allow your true family to live if you answer this question. This one little question!"

He said and stood up looking at him right into the eyes against the chair. We were all watching, wondering what was going to happen next.

"Identify any co-conspirators and spies with in the nation, and I will consider letting you live. You won't be able to be a free man- but you will have your life."

"I'd rather be dead than help the likes of you.."

"Oh my dear... you'll be dead alright.. Not only will your body die but your soul will die with it. *STRING THIS FUCKER UP!*"

The guards grabbed the man and moved down the pulleys, wrapping the rope around his ankles and feet before pulling them back up. He was now hanging upside down, and as the teacher started to rip each of the buttons off his shirt I suddenly got a bad feeling from the deep pit in my stomach.

"Unlike other prisoners, you won't have the right to mercy, or even honour.. you'll be nothing more than an insect, a toy to these children.."

He turned around, "That is unless you change your mind!"

"*FUCK YOU!*" he said. The guards looked and grinned at each other.

"Oh dear, of course.. Come on then children!!" he said taking out this covering from the desks. Over it was a long red velvet cloth, with small knives over it. They looked like the size of steak knives, but they had serrated edges on them, and there were a number of chain mail gloves over in another box he put on top of the desk.

"Come here, everyone gets a knife! Be careful and take some gloves, you don't wanna fucking cut yourself, these are sharp!"

They did seem awfully sharp and gleaming. I looked at it closely then at the man hanging upside down.

"Now cadets!! Anyone who gets to his heart first will receive and honorary metal of glory and a personal letter of recommendation from me! And if you eat it, you will get a very very special reward!!"

I gulped and turned white. Suddenly my head felt light and I could feel the room spinning. I closed my eyes and tried to relax somehow. *I'm not here, I'm somewhere else!* I thought. I*'m in a nice place, a place full of flowers and sunlight, like a meadow-*

"You shit.." Cortmon said, "You'd get children to do your dirty work for you??"

"Why not?! You're nothing but a lick of dog shit! But to these kids now, you're worth something far more. A covenant of loyalty, between this nation and God himself!" the teacher yelled.

Cortman grimaced, his face was turning red and the sweat was starting to pour down his face.

"Oh and don't go thinking that this will be a walk in the park, these knives I am told they feel like little shark teeth pecking at your body."

He looked at the students, "Oh yes, his

bones will be hard to get through so you'll really have to put some elbow grease into it!"

Most of the students got ready, I shook as I put on the glove holding my knife close to me. I didn't want to do this at all, I tried to think of something, some kind of way out of this.. maybe I could ask-

"Now, did you change your mind yet Stevie boy?! Or shall I let the sharks have at you!"

I closed my eyes in the closet thing I had to pray. Please say yes, please say yes."

"*Fuck YOU SHIT!*" he yelled.

"Alright!! Cadets Ready!! And.. go!"

The children looked all like hungry little beasts as they ran at him with their knives, slowly pecking away at his skin. The blood slowly starting to drip down as they started to yell and scream at him.

"*DIE TRAITOR!*" one of them said.

"Get his heart! His heart!!"

"That's not where his heart is dummy! It's in his chest!"

"I want it, I want it!"

I just stared there pale, as the teacher came up behind me.

"What are you waiting for Cadet Ortix?! He's not gonna chop himself up now is he!!" the teacher said so close, I could almost taste his breath on the back of my neck.

I didn't move, just held the knife close to me, hearing the man's screams as he was being slowly chopped to bits in front of us.

The teacher suddenly turned me around and I could see into his dark black eyes, and smell his aftershave.

"*RUNIE!*" he yelled at me, "You've always been a pain in my ass! There isn't a time when you haven't caused shit for me in some way or another! Now I want you to get there and see your soaked elbow deep in *BLOOD!* If I do *NOT*, I will personally give you an ass beating so bad that it will look like that man's face understand?! *DRINK HIS BLOOD!!*" he hissed and shoved me, hard into the man. I stared and shook, looking back and forward. I didn't know what to do. The students we're paying attention.

"*HELP! GOD HELP ME!*" the man screamed.

"Cadet.." the teacher stared at me. I wasn't sure what to do, I moved away from the teacher and started to try to pretend to stab, rubbing some of the blood on my blade. The blood started to splash all over the place suddenly on all of us. Someone must've cut his neck, it was squirting hot and messy. I could feel it stick against my hands. I had to do something, so I decided to grab as much as I could and plaster it all over my face and chest.

"That's more like it!" The teacher said, seeing me to this. "Get in there!!"

I pretended to rub the knife and stab him for an hour. By the time it was all said and done, the cadets were exhausted, and one was not giving up, he had his hand deep into that man's chest and pulled out a random organ.

"I got it! I got it!" he yelled.

"Well.." The teacher looked at him,

"Close enough I guess! Congratulations Jules!"

I pretended to be exhausted but really I was feeling stick. Some of the poor man's flesh even splattered over me from pecking, and I saw his corpse now, I tried to look away but couldn't. It looked like it was torn apart by some animal. His head was twisted slightly and you could see some of his spine coming through. And the smell, the smell of blood, and human waste, that sour smell that didn't escape my nose until I left that place.

I took my final report card, then headed back to my room to clean up and wash off. I didn't look at it until after, I had to get all that smell of blood and sweat off me- I was close to being sick I couldn't help it. Then I opened it.

On my reports it said had everything from academics to military courses.

Mostly B's a Cs... on my area of conduct, I got a D-. But below it said I passed. Thank god. I should've kinda figured he would let me pass. That teacher, if at any point he could be clearer of disliking me he couldn't be clearer than on that day, and I honestly didn't care. I was glad to be over with.. but something told me this wasn't going to be over. I was going back home soon and soon I would have to face my father again. I had an idea I was going to still get beaten either way, I was sure of it. But at least it wouldn't be as bad as if I failed.

I tried to think.. think of the people who all lost their lives as a result of this, of me. But I pushed it away.. I just, had to. If I didn't I knew I was going to go insane, insane from the guilt that was already starting to seep through my soul. If only I was stronger somehow, if only I could've made a difference.

I was starting to wonder what Nana would think if she knew what I did, and how disappointed she'd be as a result.. but I pushed that away too. There was nothing that could've really been done. Was there?

Was there anyway I could've prevented from those poor people being killed? I tried to stop thinking but couldn't. I started to pack things, that would help me forget, yes.

I felt glad that I was leaving this place, even though I was going back "home". It would be good to get back to do some work that didn't involve killing something.

Chapter 3

1

When I got back to the house I couldn't help but feel some measure of relief. My father didn't seem to be around. I went to inform the maids who took some of my belongings inside the maid house. They told me they didn't know what I should do and that I should only keep out of the way. I went back to the barn, changing into some old clothes and looked around. Yep, same old barn, that's for sure. Nothing seemed to have changed.

I went to sit on a little stool and sat

back, looking around and noticed something.. a strange kind of door seemed to be visible behind a bunch of hay. I looked around and wondered why was it there..?

Beside the barn was the old farm house. It was left in tatters and boarded up. Nobody went in there, and who knew what could be in there. Probably a bunch of raccoon or something, but my curiosity was peaking, and I looked about. Father was still not home yet, and nobody else was around but the chickens. So I decided to try to take away the hay and have a closer look at the door.

The door itself didn't seem to be locked, but it was hard to open. Once I managed to pull on it I almost sent myself flying back but it slowly scrapped open on the ground below and the weird smell of ancient dust and other musty things came out from the deep darkness inside. I looked inside and could see nothing but shadows and blackness.

I turned around one last time to make sure I wasn't being followed, then slowly started to descend into the darkness. There were specks of light here and there, so I didn't really need much of a flash light.

Deep down stairs I could see that webs covered almost everything, and that the strange calmness of this place though as dark as it may be, was somewhat over powering. Every once and a while a creaking noise could be heard somewhere else in the house but it was impossible anyone else could be roaming about up there.

It looked as if I was in the basement, lots of strange instruments were laid across the table, now rusted from the years of absent use. But across from there, was a shelf of something that seemed to just sort of sit in the darkness quietly. I approached it and at first couldn't believe what I was seeing. Books, dozens and dozens of them. I stared and grabbed one, it was in a language I couldn't understand. I put it back, and grabbed another, this one I could understand and seemed to be some kind of stories, a list of them. On the cover it said

"1001 Arabian Nights" I stared and pondered at this, then put it back. I decided to explore some more and in another room I found even more books and papers, stacked all over. They seemed to luckily be unharmed from the elements- I glanced over at some of the papers, they seemed to be from 50 years ago. There were such things 50 years ago? I never saw anything like this before.

Ads for cars, and railroad schedules, things of that nature. And stories about people from other regions.. still the strange nationalism that appeared in the previous pamphlets they gave were still there. But.. this, all of this, seemed most alien to me.

I glanced over at another section, there seemed to be barrels of wine and other books laying about. They were all stored in boxes and boxes one on top of the other. I looked through some, a lot seemed to be hand written- I couldn't help but wonder who could write such things- they writing seemed almost perfect and I wished that I could that kind of control with the pen to be able to write so artistically.

Just then outside, I heard something start to roll in, it was my father's car. Quickly, I put the book back and ran back upstairs almost tripping. As soon as I got back up I could see my father get back out of his car.

I tried to push the door back, but the damn thing didn't want to close tight. I pushed and pushed, it's wooden frame grinding against the floor. I could feel the draft from below coming through the small cracked that remained. I pushed again, pushed again with all my might and loudly it shut.

I quickly threw all the hay back over it, throwing the last one just as my father entered. He stared at me with cold unyielding eyes.

"Where are your papers?" he asked sternly.

I stared, and quickly took them out from my back pocket presenting them to him.

"Why are you sweating so much?"

"Huh?" I asked confused, "Uh! I was working out sir!" I said standing up straight, "I don't want to get soft during these summer months!"

"Oh, don't worry about that.." he mumbled, then looked at the report card.

It took him a minute before he sighed, and grumbled. "See, D- in conduct! CONDUCT!! I wouldn't give a shit if you were bad at math or at Yiddish- but conduct! You must carry yourself better!! When you are out there you don't only represent our country but our household!!"

"Yes sir!" I said loudly.

"Hmph. Cut the ass kissing. Who cares about that." He took the papers and put them in his own pocket and rubbed his face.

"At least you somewhat performed admirably today during the execution. But you could've done a lot better. Next time I expect you to eat that heart- understand??"

I started to shake a bit but nodded. "Sir, yes sir!"

"Now go get back to work! I want this place spotless when I come back!" he said, getting up and walking away.

I wasn't sure what he meant by spotless. The place was a damn barn, it was always going to be messy no matter what I did. But I tried to sweep and put everything away perfectly as much as I could before he came close to returning. But my mind started to wander.. about that house and the basement. About the books that were there for so long unread, and I couldn't help but get a little excited.

2

After taking care of the animals and cleaning up the barn as best as I could, my father came by to give me might nightly beating. I wiped my mouth from blood and waited until I was sure most people were in bed, then went back down into the house's basement for a closer inspection. I was lucky to have a flash light with me, but I was still worried of being noticed by anyone outside of lurking down in the basement. I could hear things and shadows move about, but couldn't really see them. As I lurked through the basement I got this odd feeling as if I was being watched, that I wasn't alone.. but I tried my best to push that away. Probably rats or something like that. I had to be brave, I had to force myself to be brave at this point.

The bravery against the darkness and what else may be lurking here, but it shouldn't be what's inside that is worrying me, it's what's outside.

I stared and turned towards the last book I seen, *1001 Arabian nights*, and took it out and began reading. I read and read so much, I didn't realize this was part one in a series. Each of the stories seemed to be rather small, but they seemed to be from strange off lands, of strange beings and things I never heard of and weird kind of relationships.. I didn't know anything about love or sex at that point in my life. I don't know if it was normal for any 8 year old to to begin with, but I did find it somewhat.. inciting.

There was more than one book, I must've read through three of them before getting sleepy and nodding off. It wasn't until the next morning I woke up and seen the sunlight I panicked. I ran back upstairs and closed the door tightly behind me, as tightly as I could force it. It must've been around 5:30am, and my heart was pounding in my chest but I felt relief I got away with it. I gotta be more careful.. maybe.. get something to wake me up, but it was beyond me what kind of device could do such a thing.

As I went through the day, sweating it out and being drenched in filth, the I relieved every single one of the adventures from the tales I read in my head and couldn't understand why anyone would be afraid of such a thing. I couldn't help but wonder what it was like, to live in the desert and be a sultana, or be someone looking for treasure, everything was just so.. pleasurable it was almost like being on a drug.

As the sun rolled back down below the

horizon, I did it again, and again the next night. I read the whole series and couldn't believe it. I almost cried at the last book, distressed there wasn't anymore added. I wanted to continue to read the adventures and what not and wished there was a way I could keep on going through this life.. But I slowly got over it, and read the next book, and the next. Some were difficult to understand, the wording was so odd. I summed it up to the fact that I was too young, too ignorant understand what was being said to me, it wasn't until much later in my life I understood that this is how differently people spoke through history.

The basement helped keep me cool during the long hot summer ahead, and helped keep me sane while being beaten to an inch towards my life when I did screw up. I asked my father if I was going back to school come the end of this summer, he said that I had enough of that. Now it was time for me to become a real soldier.. I didn't know what that meant, but I was under constant worry what it could possibly mean. Does that mean drinking the blood of my enemies? Or something else? It seems like all the horrible things I was put through my past life, was what I had to go through to be a soldier. I didn't know how absurd it really was..

That night I sat in the cool basement thinking to myself and wondering.. wondering what it meant to be in the army, to "serve". To serve what? This massive strange beast that seemed to lust for tears and blood? The horrible nightmare machine of some sort? I still had nightmares over those killings, those poor people who were slashed to pieces or bitten to bits by bullets and knives and other pointy things- teeth.

But slowly, my dreams where starting to be conquered with better ones, of going through the desert and strange things that I have read through.. even romances sometimes.

As my mind wandered and I day dreamed my eyes moved towards those barrels from before, and the written accounts of something that I seen earlier. I walked towards them and began digging through them, curious what I could find.

I took one book, it was big and fat with paper and notes, little pieces of paper that stuck out and looked ancient. I slowly began to read and as I did nothing but more questions came to my mind, about this place, about where I lived- So many questions which still remain unanswered.

Nissan 24, 5724

After this encounter, I no longer feel the willingness or curiosity to further investigate the exclusion zone. The the idea, of using this strange ethereal material for our personal use is nightmarish and unthinkable.

I returned to the area, the remaining guards there had all disappeared, no traces remain but their uniforms   and pieces of dried flesh and skin. We are working to get

*them analyzed, however I don't need to analysis
to know what happened, the dust had
took them. And now we are playing with the
idea of experimenting with it, using it in
combination with our own population for and
attempt to use it for our own means and ends.
Xeamdere called it "Oculus", after the
strange plants that grew in the exclusion zone
with eyes that stare   into your soul and follow
you around. I call it a damn abomination. I told
him I had no choice but to recommend the
complete exclusion from every day life use for
all citizens. I am sure he won't agree, he
is already taken by it. It seems like everyone
who is exposed to this chemical is shifted, their
whole being becomes a
weird kind of perverse version of their former
selves and
I am at a loss with how to return them
back to normal.
Those who have been altered,
seemed to become grotesque mutations of
something unearthly and almost demonic. We*

are pretty sure that it came from some kind of meteorite but we don't know for certain, the whole area was altered by the dust and at this point it's impossible to be sure. Xeamdere is just interested in harvesting now. Harvesting for the future. Whatever that means. I am unsure what will happen. The animals whichare exposed for too long become so altered, they no longer   resemble anything that even comes close to their previous form. What am I suppose to do with this? How am I going to possibly get rid of all these ideas and philosophy of actually using this for our own devices?

      I must find a way, a way to destroy this research.. but the power Xeamdere wields is vast, especially since his kin rules the circle at during this cycle. G-d help me. G-d help us all...

      I had no idea what he was talking about, what this "Oculus" was, or the nightmare he was talking about. I didn't even know who this guy was, why were his books in my basement. But as I continued reading, things became clearer and clearer to me, and I wish they weren't. I wished this wasn't something that I was exposed to- if only that they were right- this was a nightmare.

Nissan 25, 5724

I made a mistake. A mistake that Xeamdere had any more humanity left in him. He doesn't. He is purely interested in pushing Oculus as a medical experiment.

Experiment for what?! What kind of good would this have to do with anyone or anybody? The mutations are too strong, and now he wants to risk exposing it to everyone. I must stop him.. I must find a way to poke

holes into his work, but worse I fear for my family. If I am too aggressive I am sure he will go after them. I think they plotting against me somehow, or are losing faith in me. I'm not sure why or how, but perhaps I have also been

*exposed too long to be any more good to them.
If I am not careful, they may be exposed too.*

Nissan 26, 5724

*It has come to my attention, that the
only way to properly discredit this idea of
Oculus is to start to empower people with the
proper information. That is why I decided to
join
Xeamdere's team. Now I can hopefully effect
things through on the inside and if possible, try
to somehow effect the results if I can. In this
particularly entry I shall explain what I do
know about this drug. What I do know without
any tampering from outside groups.*

*There is an overwhelming amount of
evidence supporting the idea that "The Dust"
(IE the element which is now referred to as
Oculus) is from an extra-   terrestrial origin.
Those who are exposed to "The dust"*

experience some kind of genetic modification, regardless of how small or minute that exposure is, the effects are shown   sometimes days, or weeks after exposure but they do come up.

The mutation never stops. It continues on and on regardless of the exposure to subjects, no matter   who they are, or what they area. Animal, plant, human the mutations continue.

Those who are exposed to Oculus are shown to have some kind of altered behaviour, and almost   with inhuman qualities. No matter what the exposure is, the personality of whatever is exposed is permanently altered.

If left unimpeded, who knows what kind of exposure or use Oculus will have on our lives. Perhaps a weapons of war.. perhaps some kind of derivative of medical advice... I don't know...

Eventually those exposed will become so altered   they won't resemble anything they were originally. We   seen that with plants, and with people. Why are they pushing this so hard?

The research is limited but it is my belief this... material, should be destroyed as soon as possible. It's my only hope that if it isn't, someone who is reading this in the future will be able to see this and know the truth. The truth of Oculus, no matter what role it may play in our society for years to come...

I had no idea what he was talking about. Oculus? What is Oculus? Did it really play a big role in everything as he said? I shivered, and closed the book being unable to read anymore. This was, too strange, too real, too odd. Whatever you wanted to call it.

Maybe I should take a break and that is what I did for that night, trying to clear my mind out what I read that sounded like rantings from a madman. But then again, to me, everything seemed to be mad to me.

I spent more time searching through the documents trying to figure out who this person is, and anymore information about Oculus, however I couldn't find very much, not in the boxes that I did find.. summer was starting to wind down, and soon I would be deployed again somewhere. In a way I am sad to see it go, but I couldn't help but wonder what or where I will be sent to next. My father seemed to be mute about it, maybe I won't be going anywhere. Though the thought of freezing to death inside the barn isn't exactly something I am looking forward to.

I tried to sneak some books together in my bag before I left, hoping that nobody will see, I left the strange diaries behind though just in case. If someone did see those I'd have a much harder time explaining them.

People seemed to avoid looking through my things, though I am not sure why. I can only guess that maybe because I am a girl it makes them uncomfortable somehow? I don't know for sure- I mean it's just cloth honestly but I wasn't going to question it. I just had to keep pushing forward.

Suddenly September moved in, and I was helping with the harvest, picking and organizing them from the collector. It looked like I wasn't the only slave around here, many of them helped out when it came to harvest time.. my father finally took me by the arm and told me I was going to go off to boot camp tomorrow.

"You better not embarrass me this time!" He said, as he began his lecture, "You do what you're fucking told, and if I have to come out all the way there to beat your ass I will swear it'll be so fucking red you'll need to sit on an ice cube to keep from going crazy!"

I was lucky to have kept those strong pills, who knows when I would have to use them next.

"So get yourself cleaned up and sleep in the maid's quarters tonight, I don't need you stinking up the joint when you arrive. You better look respectable." He said, walking away. I looked somewhat disheartened.

"I do not stink up the joint.." I mumbled.

I went back inside and bathed, I couldn't believe that water could be so warm. I sat in that tub and almost melted away.. then I finally got to sleep with some long garment that the maids gave me. It felt strange and awkward, like wearing a lampshade or something. I couldn't get use to it at all, and it must've been the first dress I worn in a while, it just felt, weird.

When I went to bed, I could've sworn I never had a better sleep in my life. Even compared to the beds at the dorm, this was something on a totally different level. I must've passed out right away because I didn't remember anything until the next morning when the sun's rays slowly peaked through the curtain like a blinding beam.

I stared and looked at the clock, 5:30

am, maybe I shouldn't push it and get ready. am I suppose to leave at 7:30 or 8:30? I couldn't remember.. and when I woke up again it was 7:15am.

I panicked, and got up- I must've flung that dress over the lamp because I couldn't see it at all as soon as I took it off and got back into my dress uniform. It felt better than the dress, maybe I was just getting too use to this now.

The maids did feed me, and didn't seem to mind my presence, but I couldn't help but feel this weird, unforeseen tension in the air. Like they were expecting me to do something or they were afraid of me for some reason. I couldn't put my finger on it. And as I went out to wait for my ride, I couldn't help but notice someone was watching from the main house... the curtain there pushed aside.. who on earth could it be? My mother?

I waved, and they disappeared immediately. For a second I thought my father would come out and beat me but no, no such send off.

"Mr. Ortix..." the driver said saluting me, "I am to take you too Rainstar boot camp, sir."

I nodded, "Where is this boot camp?" I asked.

"It's not too far away, about half an hour." he paused, then gave me a small booklet. "I was told to give you this as an introduction to the boot camp."

"Is there going to be a test on this later..?" I asked, he didn't respond. Maybe he didn't hear me or he wasn't interested in responding. However, when I began to read I couldn't help but feel parallels between this and the last book I read.. About the history, the land, the people.. and the "future". It all just made me, kinda sick.

I sat back and enjoyed the ride and scenery, I had a hard time believing such a beautiful place could have such a strange underbelly. But as I started towards the city where the boot camp was located, things changed. The city looked to be in poor sorts in some places, buildings crumbling, looking abandoned. Others looked like they were hit by some kind of explosion. The, everything had weird smoke and dust coming out from every nook and cranny of places and the people looked so weary, so strange. Some did look as if they were put through the wringer, others looked as if they been hurt somehow.

"Who are these people?" I asked, as we drove through.

"Peasant class." The driver said, "Don't worry, the camp doesn't look this bad."

As the rolled further into the town the landscape changed. The roads weren't so bumpy and chewed up, they were smooth and everything looked clean. People who were walking about also looked less chewed up but it had this, strange quiet feeling. Like they were being watched somehow. I didn't notice anyone else about, everyone looked busy and seemed to be doing their own thing, nobody was shopping or laughing or enjoying anything. It was all business from what I saw.

The car finally got the the boot camp, massive wire fences surrounded it, some looked rusted and covered with blades, others just appeared to be crumbling into pieces. It seems like they just keep adding more on to it rather than taking it apart.

There were still some peasants there, sweeping and keeping their head down, but most of the guards were walking about and everyone was doing something. Everyone had their own place.

When I was left off, it was near another group of people. They were all kids my age, some looked to be talking and actually seemed happy, others were keeping to themselves and looked on the verge of crying. I wasn't sure what everyone's story was, maybe I wasn't the only one coming here against my will, but after what I've been through, I considered myself now lucky.

I went and sat close to a heart broken kid. He was just staring at the ground. I didn't talk or say anything to him, he didn't even look as if he saw me, let alone knew where he was himself. I wondered how long we were going to sit like this, and read some of the book the driver gave me earlier. On the cover it said something like this:

Camp Rainstar:
For the future

I must've said something distasteful because the other kid looked up with brightened eyes towards me. I stared, then smiled at him. He looked away shyly and didn't say anything else.

I rubbed my head, it must've been another hour until someone showed up in a jeep. He was the same kind of person I always saw around here, his stare was stern, he wore a flat brim hat, and his ace looked tomato red like he'd been screaming at someone recently.

"*ALRIGHT* you pieces of shit! Let's Line up!" He blew his whistle and it took a moment before people actually moved up in line with their backpacks and other things, trying to look as respectable as possible.

"I am Drill Sargent Xason. For the next two years you will be moulded into discipline swords of the *NATION*." He said walking and then turning back around. "When you are done those of you who are ready to be deployed to the field will be! Those who are taking specialist courses will take specialist courses!!" He paused and looked at one of the students. "What is your fucking problem!?"

"Nothing sir!" The boy said, it looked like he was scared to death. He was scared so much he was shaking.

"Then stop standing there like a fucking tree in the wind and stay still!" he said, the student nodded.

I sighed, more of this again huh? The more things changed the more they stayed the same.

"As I said, you are now in training, you will behave as if you are in training from this point forward you are soldiers to BE! So you will act like soldiers to be! Therefore, those of you who are required to get your uniforms will go through uniform and contingency checks! And when I make a statement or ask you a question, you will respond with *'YES DRILL SARGENT!!'* Is that clear?!"

"*YES DRILL SARGENT!*" I said, I was the only one and then looked embarrassed, my little heart still thumping hard in my chest.

"Holy *MOSES* Ortix you're the only one here who doesn't have their head up their ass! As expected from a Gold kin!" he said.

"Alright, let's MOVE ON out!!" he said, "*ATTEN HUT!*" he said and growled at some of the kids not knowing what to do.

"That way geniuses!" he said smacking one of them on the head.

As everyone started to move out he stopped, and pointed to two other students and me. "You, you and you- stay!"

I stood there, not surprised but wondered why other students were staying with me. I didn't noticed they too were wearing the golden patches.

"You three are members of the kin-circle. But just because you are doesn't mean I won't be any less harder on you! If you fuck up I'll be all over you like a shit on a cow's ass understand?!"

"Yes drill Sargent!" We responded.

"Good, so you better show the right conduct and courtesy and do what is asked of you, I'm looking at *YOU* Ortix!" He came to me and looked down pointing his meaty finger right near my face.

"If you fuck with me I will fuck with you. So don't try that little smart ass shit you pulled before, I know your history!"

I nodded looking at him wide eyed.

"Don't you fucking use those puppy dog eyes on me!" he said, then smacked me upside the head. I tried not to move or show any kind of distress.

"Now, go get your uniforms and building GO GO!" he said, and almost chased us down towards it.

When we got there they gave us so much equipment we could barely see where we were going. Of course I was sent away to my own room, which was nice for a change. The rooms here for us seemed comfy, a bit too good to be true really. I was expecting myself to get thrown out of here soon enough. I was wondering what the other students got but, they probably received some form of bunk beds or something.

When we did get all ready, we (as in the kin circle), were asked to join the others in the cafeteria but I was temporarily stopped by the two boys earlier who were also wearing similar gold badges to mine.

"Hey," One of the boys said, "We wanted to talk to you about something."

"Who, me?" I asked, dumbfounded.

"Yeah," the other boy said, "We just got notes saying that we shouldn't talk to associate with you in any way." They both looked sternly at each other, "What makes you so goddamn special?"

"I don't know!" I said shrugging. "I wasn't even aware of it!"

"Yeah right." the first boy said. "If you want to know how it works here, you're no better than us- even if you're better than *THEM*." he pointed down the hall, "So don't think we're gonna put up with your bullshit, understand, Ortix?" he said and flipped my hat off my head.

I stared nodding, and waited until the walked away to pick up my hat and dusted it off. So that's why nobody talked to me in class, they were telling them not to.. why? I didn't know the whole story, maybe I didn't want to know. Maybe it had something to do with me being a girl.. come to think of it didn't they mention something about that before? And everyone is calling me "Mister" and stuff..? I didn't really think too hard about it until now..

I walked back down the hallway towards orientation, hoping that this won't become a pain. It's bad enough I had to deal with the instructors, I didn't want to start dealing with the drama from my fellow students.

5

As days went further I didn't notice any difference, at least not directly. I mostly kept to myself on free time or in my room, I wasn't too interested in really meeting people that much, not that there was much free time to begin with. During mornings we'd always have drills especially if it rained. Sometimes they would just soak the earth with water just to make things harder for us to get around- most of the time when we were finished we had to take off our equipment and were forced to go clean up right away. They didn't do that for me though, just strip off everything that wasn't essential, save the pants and go dress in your room. It was a bit annoying at first but later on I considered myself lucky.

My fellow students always looked at me strangely when I came back, wondering why I wasn't cleaning up with the others I assume. I tried my best to do what was asked of me, to not cause any "trouble", there wasn't much at first but as the training went on we started using human targets.

There didn't seem to be any shortage of them either. We would either shoot or be forced to gut them with bayonets. Sometimes they even used swords- I was slowly getting use to it, I didn't have much of a choice- I knew if I didn't take part they'd end up beating the shit out of me so I had to be careful. Luckily, nobody ever gave me a hard time because of that.

If anything the hardest time of the day was lunch time. The one time I couldn't go back to my room to eat or anything. They all shoved us into the hall at noon and made us usually eat things that I considered to be, inedible. Sometimes you could smell the rancidness off the food they were giving us. They said it was to "harden" our bodies, so that we could be use to eating whatever it took to survive. I didn't know if that was true or not, but I tell you later on it certainly didn't feel true when I got stomach cramps as a result of it.

One time when I was heading towards to find some place to eat, it seemed like none of the golden kins wanted to share.

"This place is taken." they'd normally say, until I found a table with barely nobody sitting at it, three other students. I didn't even ask, I just sat down. One of them came up to me and stared me down, and said: "We don't allow little faggots like you into our circle, even if you are gold."

I stared back and ignored them. All I wanted to was to relax.. I had a tough day at that point, and even if they were from different families other than mine- but they still wore those golden badges as I did. I wasn't sure what to do, but I was starting to get annoyed.

"Hey, you listening to me?" He said, grabbing my hand. I glared back down at him, and something must've snapped. I don't know what I was thinking- I just acted on pure instinct.

I grabbed the fork and for a moment, I was only going to threaten him with it- I didn't even want to hurt him. But something just jumped in me, I moved and stabbed him with it right in the face.

It got him right into the cheek and he growled, pushing my food out of the way and threw me on the floor.

"You little bitch!! I'm gonna fucking kill you!" He said, then stared to punch me. I didn't do anything- I was too much in shock that I actually did that too. It took a few moments, I don't know how long but then another man came up behind him and pulled him off. It was someone with the same cast, golden badge- different shape.

"Let me fucking go!! Look what that little shit did to my fucking face!" he said screaming at the teacher.

"That's nothing compared to what I'll do to you if you don't calm your shit down!" he said, glaring at the boy. "Now get your ass to the infirmary and stop being such a whiny bitch!"

He almost pushed the boy along, and looked down at me. Blood was coming from my mouth and nose and he just shook his head.

"Well- at least you did something to him-" he said. "Go see the doctor on the west side of the building."

The others stared at me as I walked off, trying to wipe the blood away from my face. I didn't eat after wards, all they gave me was some ice to put on my cheek. But I was more disturbed by the fact I lost my temper, and such a cruel way. What was I thinking? How could I do such an awful thing..? I never did anything like that before. It was at that point I promised myself, I would never lose my temper again no matter what. I would always be happy- just push it down, all the way down until it doesn't matter anymore.

That night I still felt ashamed of myself. I needed to get my mind off the awful events that happened today so I decided to read a bit more before going to sleep, the novel I got was massive. It seemed to be about a man who was desperate for revenge after being convicted of a crime he didn't commit.

I was wondering what could've compelled someone to write such a book in the first place- did something similar happen in their life too? It wasn't as enjoyable or as magical as the first books I read, but it was quite captivating compared to most of the other material they had in the boot camp.

I must've fell asleep afterwards, because I was having my own strange dream that I was convicted for something I actually did do- reading books.

Of course I denied it, but there was nothing I could do- and was sent to a similar place in the book- only instead of seeing an old man there it was a corpse of bones and shredded cloth.

It was quiet for a moment, but then the skeleton started to talk to me..

"Don't stop.." it said in a strange kind of

gravely voice.

"Huh?"

"Don't stop... Never stop." it said, before it started to crawl towards me from the shadows. It was starting to get a little scary now, the room was growing dark- everything was turning dark... "Continue on..!" it said as it grabbed me and started to crawl up my legs.

I screamed in my dream and woke up, it was still dark.

"Stupid dream.." I said, trying to go back to sleep. I didn't know what it meant. But maybe thinking back now I always knew what it was.

6

Several weeks passed without incident. The training was starting to get a bit more intense as we started to cover some kind of strange marital art called "The Path". Apparently it was created by a team of doctors to help manipulate the most weakest parts of the human body and to push enemies into submission.

"The Path is an extremely easy to learn, but hard to master. Of course, at this point in your lives you will not be able to come anywhere close to mastering it. But it doesn't hurt to learn it even if you aren't capable of using it at it's full potential."

Most of it seemed to be manipulating sensitive areas like the eyes, nose, groin, etc..

I was never too keen on mastering it- and it didn't seem to be that too many people wanted to go up against me. Compared to them I was kind of taller so I guess in some cases this proved to be a bit intimidating. Too bad that wouldn't last though.

It was incredibly hard to spar with others and not hurt them, we were instructed not to use "deadly" techniques on other students- but the teacher did show some of the more effective moves on prisoners who seemed to be half dead or dying of what I could only guess was malnutrition.

"As you can see, I have the enemy pinned on the ground." he said, the prisoner whining and trying to struggle fruitlessly underneath him.

"It's extremely easy at this point to cause damage to the prisoner, for instance- their collar bone is one of the easiest places to break on their body- just apply a little pressure like this.." He moves and snapped his hand on the man's collar bone and broke it rather quickly, of course the man screamed in pain as this happened.

"And the move has been accomplished-" he said, "Now if you really want to cause damage-" I sorta drifted off at this point, thinking of the dream I had earlier with the skeleton and wondering if any of these moves would work against creatures like that. Probably not, dreams have a funny way of not working out for anyone.

Afterwards I was walking back out from the gym hall when I suddenly encountered some other boys I recolonized from before. I was going to turn around but was suddenly stopped when someone grabbed me from the cheeks and threw me to the wall. It was that boy from before who I stabbed in the face.

"Nice seeing you again faggot-" the boy said as he held me against the wall.

"Look, I'm sorry for what happened-"

"Sorry? Does it look like sorry is going to fix this..?" he pointed to the scar on his cheek as the other boys suddenly grabbed me. I tried to move now but it was too late, I was stuck.

"W-well, what do you think will work for you?"

"I think you know, the old saying, eye for an eye-? You cut up my face- so I'm going to cut up yours-"

"Ar-are you sure this is a good idea..?"

"Are you sure this is a good idea he asks!" the other grinning heavyset boy said sneering at me.

"Do you even know my name? Do you even know any of us??" he asked, I shook my head.

"My name is Matthew. MATT-HEW. Understand?"

"Matthew, I understand-" and someone pulled my hair from behind nodding my head for me.

"Good, because I don't want you to fucking forget it- you know, how about you remember, every time you take a piss??"

"Huh?" I asked confused- the others laughed and mocked me for saying this. "What do you mean?"

"What do I mean- you think I know what you mean. We all know why you don't shower with us, or why you weren't checked out for 'contingency'." He said, taking out a rather large looking knife.

My expression must've changed, though I don't remember it changing.

"There that's what I'm talking about- the look of FEAR on your face! That's what I want to see-"

"I don't know what you're talking

about!"

"Shut up faggot! Doesn't he sound like a little fag?? You suck dicks huh fagala??"

The person who hand a hold of my head made me nod again and I grimaced at the tugging.

"I'm gonna make sure you understand.. you think your dick is so better than all of ours?? Let's see just how different you are after I give you the same job that we All had to get in this army. Then you can go whine to your daddy about how we gave you the same cut we all had!"

"Hold him-" he said, as the gathered me up tightly, so tight I couldn't move. He grabbed my belt buckle and began undoing my pants.

"Now comes the fun part.." he said holding his knife. He grinned and pulled them down. I closed by eyes and didn't want to know what was going to happen next. I tried to get way but couldn't.. blood began to draw away from my face-

"Alright now get ready to-" he began

and stopped, "Huh?"

There was silence as he stared down, looking as if he was staring at something he couldn't quite get his head around.

"What the fuck??" He said looking up at me.

"What is it? Another boy said-"

"He's a girl!! A gir-"

Suddenly someone else came around the bend- it was the drill Sargent. He didn't seem to know what was going on at first, but when he saw me with my pants down, boy he looked pissed.

"Drill Sargent! Did you know Runie was a g-" Matthew began but never got a chance to finish his sentence. The Drill Sargent grabbed him by the head and swung him right into the wall. The other other students let go and appeared to be in shock as to what he did. He grabbed another one and punched him in the gut so hard he threw up instantly. Then removed what looked to be some kind of bat and swatted the other boy right into his side.

"Look what you've done you slut!" he
said, slapping me so hard my nose broke- I
looked back at him and cried out in confusion.

"I didn't do anything!" I said defiantly.

"I don't give two rat shits what you did
or didn't do! It doesn't fucking matter anymore-
you sir are FUCKED." he said, and grumbled.

"Now get your fucking pants on you
whore before anyone sees you! We need to get
this place cleaned up!" he said. I stared in
silence as I watched him walk away angrily
from me. I never was anymore confused or
afraid in my life than at that moment.

7

My father wasn't joking about beating
me until I couldn't sit down. That's exactly what
he did. It was bad enough that I could barely
breathe through my broken nose- now it felt
like hot iron welds were all over my behind and
I couldn't sit down. Lucky I still had some of

those strong pills from before and took one. I wasn't sure exactly what would happen if I took two, but it said "as needed" so I guess I wasn't too worried.

I didn't see Matthew after that at all, in fact I didn't see any of the boys associated with what happened. I was still confused as to what he planned to do with that knife but I guess I should count myself lucky I wasn't a boy.. whatever that meant. I had no idea about the uh, workings of male and female body parts at that point- nothing really made sense to me.

The other students didn't give me as a hard a time after that. I never faced another incident, but they still treated me rather coldly afterwards. And now here I was in my room, staring off into space again wondering where the hell I will be next year at this time. Maybe I will have to deal with this problem all through my life. I sure hoped not, once was enough.

I tried to read my book but couldn't- all I managed was to drift off in odd dreams where I saw myself flying through space again- seeing things that shouldn't be seen- no that demanded not to be seen. I don't remember what they were exactly, but they were in the dark places, the lurking places- and it hurt to look at them.

When I finally arrived to this one place, it looked like a beautiful ball of blue- with seas of green and nice white puffy clouds. But then something was coming towards it- a large massive ball of fire- it looked to be happening slow and fast at the same time- but once it crashed into it the blue was turned to black- all the forest became like a giant sea of flaming magma and the planet was torn to pieces.. Slowly though, it mended itself together.. very slowly, it didn't look as beautiful before but eventually the blue water returned, and the green seas- but it had this massive jagged surface around it. I couldn't understand what this all meant when I woke up and didn't remember again for sometime later but I was starting to think taking these pills again might not be such a good idea.

Chapter 4

1

After I finally came back home I was 10 years old, and for the first time in a while I was able to read some new books from the stash in the basement. I was so relieved I cried as I opened the first book I seen in a while. The world seemed so dark, and so bleak but when I read everything came back to life.

This time I decided to take one from a different pile, the first one, it was called "Genesis", it seemed to be some kind of creation tale. It talked about god and the creation of earth and what not. I wasn't sure if I believed it, but it was pretty interesting compared to what I was reading before- and for my own mind it kind of gave a basis of creation of how things might've happened. Of course, like I said, I was only 10 at the time. I had no real idea of the history of this earth, but when the books suddenly took a turn towards a place called Egypt and Israel that's when things started to get interesting.

I could count the number of things that I knew about Israel with my single hand- all I knew it was an enemy state that wanted to use us as slaves for some unknown reason. There was mention of the Kingdom of Judah as well- and the Amaleks- which, according to the booklets- were hideous beings that sucked the blood from people.

They were all over, and sometimes they looked like normal people but they could change shape. They could look like "us", and then my mind went back to the entries of "Oculus" and I shuttered.

I wasn't sure if I believed in such things, if there was anyone who was an Amalek though it'd be my father- that was the one thing that was ever present in my mind. And the more I thought about it, the more it made sense. Everyone seemed to be "wrong", for some reason- I just couldn't explain it, in my gut it felt *wrong* and there was no other way to prove it.

In the beginning god created the heavens and the earth. He said "Let there be light" and there was, then separated light from darkness. Good from evil, was that it? Was darkness that which was evil..? But there is so much of it, compared to the light, it's all encompassing, and the stars in the sky look like little specks of white in the sky during the night.

That's what it feels like. Being in a sea of darkness and burning so bright everyone else turns on you when you try to do something you *know* is wrong.

Maybe I'm really crazy. Maybe it's me who is evil, I'm just evil in a good world that is trying to right me and that I should try to give up and go the right way. So why does it feel so sickening when I try to turn around and do the "right" thing? What makes my stomach churn so badly and why?

Maybe I'm just crazy.. maybe I don't know what it means to be good or evil, and I didn't even have an idea until this "Satan" character showed up in the book.

Satan, or Lucifer, or whatever you want to call him, didn't unquestioningly obey god, he did question his power and was paid for it eventually. I didn't know exactly what was the sin that was so bad he committed. Is questioning someone's authority bad enough to simply get them banished into a sea of flame? It looked that way to god- so why did it matter to him so much? I didn't know, I couldn't understand it and it was hurting my head.

So the devil gave Eve this piece of fruit from the tree of "knowledge", is knowledge evil? Is it something that cannot be forgiven once obtaining it?

I closed the book and stopped reading, I wasn't sure what I was getting from this but thoughts were going through my head. I kept on though, and wondered if the knowledge I was gaining right now was an act of evil? That's what made me question myself and question things around me. Maybe my Father was right, and this churning feeling in my soul was just the evil leaving my body, but it sure didn't feel like it. And now I was sitting here stuck in it, I read the book and there were various more tales that came from the book, Cain and Abel, the tale of Moses and the Jews.. and mentions of being the chosen people of God.

The chosen people of God? But why? That's a phrase I heard a lot in all the booklets and propaganda they forced on us. We were anointed by God to lead this world..Lead them to what? I didn't know, I didn't want to know.. I put the book down at the end and just felt more conflicted. As I read more and more books things came together a bit more.. but it didn't come easy. I read the Testament, Revelations, the Talmud- the talk of the Messiah who would come and save us, and I couldn't help but wonder what was taking him so long. If there was anytime or any place where people needed help it was this place right? I didn't know.. I wasn't sure whether to believe it or not because it seemed to be so serious and took itself so seriously. There were other books too from languages I couldn't understand, but out of all of them, stood this strangest of the strange.

Two books. Both found at the bottom of this old steel chest. It looked like there could've been a lot on it at some point.. but it was smashed long ago.

One book, was wrapped in chains and fabric. It looked like it was in a box.. but on it it said. "ABSOLUTELY DO NOT OPEN- DO NOT READ" on it. The other one, was in a box sealed with black wax, a lock on the side of it. I'm not sure why there was so much wax on it.. I tried my best to open it but the lock looked extremely heavy and didn't seem as if it wanted to give at all. There was nothing else on it, no message, nothing that I could see.

I shook the large box and thought I felt something in there. Why would they keep it if it was so dangerous? Perhaps some kind of weird, device was in it- maybe it wasn't a book at all.

I wasn't detoured though- I wanted to open that box and looked around for any keys that might fit. None of them did- one did actually seem as if it would fit but.. at the last minute it refused to open.

It didn't work on the forbidden book either.

Okay, what should I do now? I thought while looking at the book, Can't seem to break the lock, the key isn't down here.. maybe it's upstairs? There could be more books up there too. I thought for a moment, and decided to save it for another day.. Not to mention if they saw someone with a flash light going up and down they may expect someone had gotten in. And then I'd lose everything- everything! I couldn't stand the thought of that anymore not now.

That was suddenly a secret fear in the back of my mind. If they ever found this place or maybe they would burn it down or something just by chance. I pushed these in the back of my mind though. I had to, I had to ensure though this place was protected somehow.

As I worked the next morning I couldn't help but feel things coming easier. Maybe it was because I was actually putting on muscle or something as a result of what was going on or maybe I was just getting use to it.

But I couldn't help continue thinking about those damn books and the boxes, what about the boxes?

I decided that I was going to find out one way or another what was in those books. Assuming they were actually books. The forbidden one seemed to be the most interesting of them all, and I wondered if it had anything to do with the government and the relation to god. Maybe some kind of finalization of the documents I read before.. who knows?

I knew though I had to find the keys somewhere. And before the sun did set on that day when I could I went up in that house.

Trying to find the key somewhere. It was dusty but bright, there was cloth and cobwebs all over, and strange paintings of strange people wearing odd outfits. I wondered if these people were related to me- or maybe it was something else all together. I didn't recognize a single one.

Despite the dust it was a lot more comfy up here. Everything looked clean, but it also looked untouched. Like someone just put a big cloth over everything and left it here for decades.

There didn't seem to be any keys though anywhere. There were plates and shiny things- things that looked fragile like if you were to touch them they'd fall apart. I didn't want it to look as if anyone was here. I crept up the stairs to the second floor, it was even stranger here- the paintings had eyes that seemed to follow you all over, everything was in velvet and the doors themselves looked dull and dusted over. I checked every room, one was covered in so many clothes, I had a hard time finding my way around.

You can call me crazy if you want but I swear I saw one of them move too, even though it just ended up being a hat rack.

Stop being such a big scaredy cat Runie! I told myself and kept on searching. Looking in the nightstands, in the dresser. I didn't find anything but dust and chewed up cloth.

I sighed, it didn't seem like I was going to find anything up here. As I went back into the hall I looked up and saw a strange panel on top of the ceiling. It looked like it had a hook on it.

What was that for? I thought. I looked around, maybe if I- and as soon as I thought about it it was there. A long stick with a little hook on the end of it. It must've been made for this panel.

I moved up and had to jump to get it hooked on, pulling the panel forward. As soon as I did the panel opened and something came and hit me in the face. For a moment I thought it was furniture, but it was actually a ladder that was connected to the panel. It just fell out instantly as soon as I pulled on it.

I looked at my watch. It wouldn't be long now, I had to hurry up.

Moving upstairs I glanced around in the attic. It was dark and dusty up here too, like the basement. I never really saw and attic before this though and it made me wonder if there is anything good up here either.

I ducked and dodged the spiderwebs trying to find my footing- my leg must've hit the wrong board because as soon as I stepped on it it went inward and caused the board to spring up. It almost hit me in the face again actually. Why did that keep happening? I must be a huge klutz to keep on falling for that again and again.

I tried to move my foot out from the board and as I did it hit something like it got stuck in there.

"Shit.." I said, and looked around worried, maybe there was something.. I saw a small iron crowbar on the side of a pillar and grabbed it- it was just in range. Carefully, I

managed to get my foot out and just barely
pulled it back up without getting cut. But there
was something in there.. a little red coloured tin
box. I moved down into the dirt and dust and
picked it up hearing something rattling in it.

"....no." I said, cocking my eyebrow.

I stared and removed the box. There was
a single key in side, the same colour as that
lock on the large box covered with wax.

It couldn't be right? I mean, this wasn't
possible for me to get this lucky. I didn't want
to waste anymore time though, and placed
everything back where it was before, taking the
tin with me and closing the panel to the attic.

As I made it down stairs I could see the
light slowly drain from the landscape I was
totally unaware how this night would be a night
to change my life forever.

2

When I got back to the basement I
eagerly cut away the wax that was caked on the

side of the box and opened the lock. Inside was this weird smell of wildflowers and ash, like something was burned in there. It was hard to tell what but there was nothing in there but a plain large book. The book itself looked like it was covered in leather and bound by iron latches. Inside the book seemed to have large sheets of paper with decorative drawings that looked odd and perhaps even nightmarish. But still they had a certain appeal for them- like something too fantastical to be imagined.

Inside the page cover read the title of the book in bold strangely printed letters that stuck up from the paper. The design inside the lettered title looked like a strange kind of vine I never saw before, and the word looked almost incomprehensible:

Necronomicon

Written by: Abdul Al-Hazred

What is this written in, another language? I thought, and was slightly disappointment. I couldn't read any of this! What a waste of time. I sighed and opened to the next page, the writing was so small I had a hard time to read it at first until I added more light to it.

I continued to read the book trying to carefully understand what was being said to me, but it wasn't particularly easy for my 10 year old mind to understand what it was being told...

Though you have obtained this sacred text from what means I am unsure of, I must warn you that you are about to embark on a path of no return. Once you begin to read this text your sanity will be threatened. I urge you that if you have no choice in the matter or if you are that unabated by your curiosity continue. Otherwise stop now, and do not open this book again.

I didn't come all this way to be stopped simply by a warning, especially when it seemed like everything was destined to me to the key to open this book, so I continued.

This book is not just a lexicon of spells. It tells about origins of those who came to earth who still lurk here and the powers that be that are still manipulating the fabric of space and time. It is not a fictional nor is it an account of farce- it is based in reality. The cold reality and truths which human-kind longs for, is not something I recommend nor do I encourage you to fully explore this lexicon. It is up to you for the purposes you wish to employ it. I am not your moral compass. However, I will urge a warning, the Outer Gods and Great Old Ones do not look upon foolishness with mercy. Their punishments are harsh and unavoidable.

Use it with caution as I continue to explain the beginning and the end to you. Read this book to know the Great Old Ones and the

Outer Gods. Know them for knowledge is the key to their power, and yours.

This whole thing sounded like one massive warning that maybe I should've taken more seriously. But I wasn't, I was eager and stupid and wanted to know what was so great about this book. I continued on just trying to skip over the parts where the author kept telling me "don't continue."

But part of me started to wonder, exactly who this guy was talking about. "*Great Old Ones*"? "*Outer Gods*"? I thought there was only one god- and he created the whole universe- that's what I was told in the original book I was reading- and this book came from the same pile, so they must've been linked together somehow. I thought for a moment trying to assess this information but then continued to read:

In the Beginning there was Azathoth. In the end there will be Azathoth.

Azathoth, the Blind. The Sleeper. For he who lurks in the centre of totality- of reality more real than that which we can possibly think we can observe with our pathetic senses can provide.

Azathoth does not love. Azathoth does not care. It only is. And will continue to be long before after we parish into dust and give way from old to new. Azathoth is beyond this, because in every single second of it's unabashed dreaming is an eternity for us-it has always been and always will be. There is no way around that.

We can't possibly think we are outside or inside Azathoth.

Because he sleeps and we are the dream. The dream of unending nonsense which spreads throughout this cosmos. When Azathoth wakes, it will be our end. Because Azathoth must remain sleeping. He sits at the centre of it all, being lulled to sleep by guardians who continue to play the instruments of madness to ensure he will always sleep. Always dream. Because his dream is our reality.

I stopped reading, more confused than I was before. Was this guy really serious about what he was writing? Or was this just a massive lure, a joke. This being known as Azathoth is suppose to be god, and is just dreaming. So our reality is a dream, then I am part of that dream. What part of dream could I play? Was this some kind of cruel joke? It felt that way. Maybe he was right, this did feel like, someone's joke. My whole life at that point felt like someone's joke. And the point of a god, a god that was merciless and cruel, or a god that didn't care about our existence. Was there a choice between such two beings?

Calm down Runie, you're thinking too much, just stop worrying and continue.

The more I read about Azathoth the more I started to wonder and question myself. It was like it was seeded there, that doubt was always seeded there. And now someone just came and casually mentions that it's a dream. I suppose I have to take it. I have to take all of it like I always did.

I sighed and read on. Wondering exactly what else could wait for me in this book. I didn't know why, I suppose it was all the hard work I did to get this damn thing at this point.

Where Azathoth ends, Yog Sothtoh begins. For he is the universe. He is reality and the fabric of space time. He and Azathoth are the same. They both occupy the same

space and time and reality. Yog Sothoth does not sleep.

Yog Sothoth is always watching. He is always watching and waiting. He is the gate way between worlds as we   know it. Realities. The cosmos itself. He is also the key.

The key to unlock the gate between our pathetic realities and dreams which lurk inside Azathoth.

I stopped. My head was starting to hurt, not to mention the feeling of being watched was slowly creeping on me. Like there was someone looking over my shoulder reading. Though I knew I was alone in the darkness I couldn't help but feel a shiver up my spine. I looked at my watch. My God it was almost 1am. I better stop. I have to wake up early tomorrow again for god knows what. Or gods know what. Who the hell knows.

I put the book back into place and wiped the wax from the table, then headed back to where I found a small mattress laying on the floor. I paused but decided against it. If I were to wake up too late here it could mean the end of the books which I gathered. If I woke up there late a beating was all I would get.

I went back up to the barn and slept, almost in a strange kind of malaise like fever. I felt myself almost spin away from my consciousness and at that moment I stared at myself. This felt real didn't it? It felt true and part of the realism which for the most part kept me anchored in the ground.

I don't know where I was, but the stars around me looked strange, not normal. And they didn't feel normal. They felt, somewhat judging. Like this whole place was a court of judgment. And there I heard weird noises that were in the distance from me. I paused, and glanced over from where I came. It was nothing but massive chains and a platform. A platform which stretched and moved upward and down. That's the thing about this place, orientation was totally and completely pointless here. As I glanced I saw something that looked like a giant sun in front of me, but the light waned and grew, almost like a heart beat. It was hypnotizing.

From there I could suddenly see something beside me. It was hard to describe what I was looking at. It looked like a beast that had a trunk, at the same time it had more that one set of eyes. They looked almost insect like. The numbers of hands it had and it was holding something. I'm not sure what it was, a pipe or something. And it was just staring at me like it never saw me before. Which is true because I never saw anything like this thing in my life. It seemed to also be wearing some manner of clothing. I'm not sure what though, it looked like, weird kind of tapestry of things around it. I paused and opened my mouth to ask it something, but at that point it just walked away in the darkness.

That's when I heard the noise from it get louder and louder, and the platform moved closer to the centre of this strange kind of burning chaos in front of me. I thought for a moment I heard a whisper or someone else- but it made no sense. Then there was more whispers, and more whispers, and talking and screaming and people wailing in joy and ecstasy and pain and horror. It was all coming into my head at once- And the NOISE- the sound of these weird kind of horns and insane flutes that just beat through my ears. I felt my head pulsating- like my brain was about to blow from everything being fed. It was all just static-

static from the outside of the universe- but I swear I could hear every single note in my head and from that moment the weird feeling I felt- the insanity like I didn't know where to look or where to go.

And I was absorbed into this light. This strange light that seemed to be dark and bright at the same time, and I couldn't move anywhere- and as soon as it was there it was gone- the whole area around cooled and went dark. And I was back in the barn again. I looked around confused, not sure what happened. Was that a dream? Or- no it had to be a dream right? What else could it be? But it felt so real. And my head, it still ached. I sat my head down again on the hay and looked up at the stars. A million tiny little sets of eyes staring down at me judging me. I couldn't take it, I closed my eyes and covered my head, trying to go back to sleep.

3

The next days were kinda muddled. It

felt like it was hard to think. Everything felt kinda hard to do, and all I wanted to do was go back to sleep. Of course I couldn't do that with my father always complaining at me so I continued on to do my job as poorly as I could get away with. Which is what I normally learned.

I also found out I will be going back to the base and coming back on and almost weekly basis. This was kind of good, and I played with the idea of taking that book with me. Even though it was a bit big, I think I could get it pass everyone without knowing.

I couldn't help but continue to think of that dream and each time I saw that strange being in my mind, that thing with the trunk, my whole body felt numb ass if it was going to fall asleep. I was so relaxed when the end of the day came I went right to bed right away. But I didn't dream. I didn't dream for the next coming weeks at all. All it was was a faded kind of, fog of sleepiness.

The day to day grind of boot-camp

wasn't too bad for me to deal with. But my mind always went back to that damn dream, so much so it was starting to become madly annoying. I continued to read the Necronomicon and was starting to learn about the other gods and beings that lurked in between the pages. But there wasn't just that, there were spells as well.

I didn't know what spells were, but I found out they were some kind of mystical incantations for summoning these things and I wondered what would happen if I actually did it. If I got away with summoning one of these beings- maybe they could come and wipe this place clean of all the garbage that seemed to dominate this "reality".

But something inside me spoke and was totally against it. This strange me, this part of me that said "DON'T DO IT." Like the marking on that other book that screamed "DO NOT READ".

"After 6 months you will be sent to your first post," my commanding officer said as I stood there somewhat unsteady. "At that point you will be a Junior grade soldier."

I nodded while standing in the office, then asked. "Any idea where I will be sent?"

My C.O. Shook his head, "No, not at that point, we're still working this out. But keep doing what you're doing and we'll see maybe if we can't even get you a choice between a set of assignments for you."

Keep doing what I'm doing? You mean just bumbling around in a stupor between myself and the outside world? I suppose that was true. I was on autopilot now and I was just ignoring what I'm saying.

Go to this and go get that. Yes sir.

Shoot that man right there in the chest. Yes sir.

Get down and give me 20. Whatever you say.

It was easy to do, and I felt a bit better about it in retrospect but in another sense I also felt terrible. I didn't remember what I did most of the day and I didn't want to remember.

Maybe that was enough for everyone around me but it wasn't enough for me. Not at this point anyway at least.

4

I did get news of my new assignment. I wasn't sure what I was looking at the first time I seen the paper. The location was some 200 miles away, in a place I never really heard of, though it was part of the country: Exclusion Zone 54. What the hell is an "Exclusion Zone"? I tried to look at any other information the provided but they said nothing. I wanted to call my Commanding Officer but of course, I was forbidden access to a phone unless it was absolutely necessary. It was really irritating.

I thought for a moment that the books inside the basement may have had something, then I remembered; exclusion zone... wasn't that mentioned in that diary about that so called "Oculus"? I looked it up, I was right. Exclusion Zone.. but there was no number mentioned. So what kind of zone was this? Did it have anything to do with this alien plant? I read some more and some more, looking through other diaries. There was more mentions of Oculus but nothing about an exclusion zone 54. How exhausting.

I grumbled and waited until next day, then finally, finally I was able to ask my C.O. About it.

"You will be brief upon arrival, I thought I made that clear last time we spoke." he said as he walked down the hallway.

"I'd just like to have some idea to know what I am dealing with before I arrive, so I can prepare."

"Prepare?" he stopped and looked at me, "You're a junior soldier now, you must always be prepared regardless! Every minute of every day for anything."

"Exactly." I said, "And I can't be unless I'm given a bit more information-"

"Okay, fine. The Exclusion Zone is a result of a struggle within it due to insurrectionists. We have isolated it to control anyone who may want to leave or get out. I'm not sure what your exact mission will be, but I am sure that will be given to you on your arrival. Be ready, next week from Thursday!" he said. That gave me a lot of time to prepare, or at least I thought it did. Instead they gave us pointless busy work, running around doing exercises like jumping about on a quarter horses and other things. It was frustrating. But I calmed myself by reading more and more of that book.

The more I read, the more I felt the need to go on. And I wondered what I would do after wards.. what will I have to look forward to when I'm done this? I suppose the other forbidden book.

I tried to find something. Anything about anymore exclusion zones in the diaries that were written, and I did finally come across one entry.

It was about the relationship between the outside world and others, the part of the diary which talked about a exclusion zone called "newline".

Apparently Newline was the name given to it from the original name "New Petra". It was mostly an experimental area to try to see what effect it would have, how people would be have if they were truly isolated from the outside world.

"They were fed lies.." the book said. "The lies they were fed were they were told that the area outside was totally destroyed and constantly under attack by the Amalek Empire. The empire, was ran by a mad king who demanded the blood of every non-amalek person there was, and we were the ones who were killing them. We were told to make the attacks as gruesome as possible to frighten the public there into obeying us without question, and it worked for a time. There were no castes there, no one was better than anyone and even some of the public took part in the "resistance" against the empire itself. They were also told more strange lies, lies about Amalek being able to change shape into things, look exactly like us, but they weren't.

"We were able to kill a whole lot of them just by putting in the seed of suspicion, though some fought back those who did were also branded to be the enemy.

"Soon however, outside many of us started to question what the point of all this was, and figured that there would be no point in continuing this experiment. However, many of the heads of state assumed that if they were to find the truth they would never forgive the true heads of state. So everyone within Newline would have to be killed as a result. Therefore, the more humane thing to do was to let them simply continue to believe the lie.

"Humane. That is the first time I ever heard such a word used by the circle. But it isn't unusual that they would use such a phrase for their own purposes."

I stopped, then pondered, maybe this is all just fiction. Maybe this was all something someone made to make me believe in false facts. But the purpose of the exclusion zone 54-insurrectionists? It all seemed to be a bit too familiar. Maybe 54 was newline.. but they would probably tell me wouldn't they? Who knows. I was just a stupid child then. They could tell me anything and I would be forced to believe it right? I grumbled. I didn't like this. I took the rest of the diary with me along with the Necronomicon and put it in my pack sack.

I thought.. and thought. How was all of this connected. The Necronomicon, the books in the basement, the diaries, the exclusion zone-Oculus It was enough to give me a headache.

That night I slept with thoughts in my head that didn't want to go away. I had no strange dreams though, just the usual. Giant strawberries everywhere with weird kinda butterflies and what not, things like that. But when I woke up, it was still dark out- I looked at the diary again.. then thought.. insurrectionist.. 54. How many exclusion zones were there? Maybe there were a lot more than I thought, however I had no real idea how big the country was- how massive or tiny it could be. They never really explained it to me.. it seemed to be on a need to know basis and I didn't need to know.

5

When the day finally came, an officer picked me up on the way to the train station. It was my first time on the train and it seemed so fancy on the outside, inside though it was a different story. It looked like there were metal seats and everything looked rusted and used. Still, I was surprised and kind of excited. I sat beside the window to stare outside- it didn't take long for the car to be filled and when it was, it felt a bit claustrophobic.

Soon the train finally began to move, chug, chug, chug.. and the sound became faster and faster it was pretty cool! I was glancing outside at all the trees going by and completely forgot about my mission to this strange unknown territory.

The train ride took four hours in all, I didn't think it would take so long. But then again they didn't really specifically tell me where I was going. Soon as we reached the city, I noticed how grey and mucky it all was. The towers of smoke stacks dominated the city, and cloudy the blue sky. People seemed to be somewhat destitute, and didn't really look anywhere but to the street- except for the guards which were all at attention all the time.

The soldiers poured out the doors from the train, I waited until last, I had no real drive to get off the train before anyone else, in fact I was kind of hoping it would take off with me still on it. Of course that didn't happen and when I did arrive I did finally get my assignment.

It was pretty simple basically- "to keep the facility up to peak and pristine standards." So pretty much cleaning duty. They brought me 4 hours here just to clean? I guess I was kind of good at it. But still it didn't seem to be the most exciting task among those which I could've been granted.

I managed to get back to my quarters, which were small, but cozy. There was a small window and a desk. It was more like a shack. There were some curtains and a small bed, nothing else. It looked like the bathroom facilities were located outside but I was told to use the ones inside the building which were frankly a lot more nicer.

The next day I was told to take turns cleaning the inside of the hallway. They wanted it to be mirror like in finish- all the time. Maybe that sounds easy to some people, but around the area of the building was extremely muddy. There were no gravel roads, no grass, just miles and miles of grey mud. I really wondered sometimes if it was mud because the smell was awful, but I didn't want to imagine anything else.

To be honest this had to be the dullest assignment ever. I suppose that was better than going around killing people so I counted my blessing to ensure that I didn't really get the chance to see anyone dead. Back at boot camp there wasn't a day that went by that we didn't see someone killed, now it hadn't happened for weeks. Trying to stay awake near the hallway was kind of painful. However, whenever people walked in and out we were told to clean it immediately- I was with one other boy- we were forbidden to speak to each other due to conduct which was okay- I wasn't feeling too much like a talking mood. I was pretty use to it.

During the nights I would continue to read the Necronomicon and the spells that were in it. They were all demanding on sacrifice and certain spells required certain locations and incantations I just couldn't provide. Sometimes they required a mountain top of forest area, something I obliviously couldn't get away to. Other times they required things I had no idea how to get a hold of.

"What's semen?" I asked while reading the book one night.

However the feeling of paranoia did seem to get stronger now, now it felt like I was constantly being watched by someone and sometimes it felt they were right behind me, breathing down my neck. This was particularly bad at work, once I turned around so fast my head almost went into the wall, the boy next to me giggled then straightened up as soon as I glanced back at him. I had no idea what was going on but I knew I had to finish that book.

Right now I was at the chapter of a being known as "Nyarlathotep" (I really hope I am spelling that right), who seemed to enjoy taunting humanity somehow by showing them unexplained things that could possibly rip apart their sanity. That fit several people I knew... but still as I read on I discovered he was also the messenger of the god being Azathoth and even Yog Sothoth- though his reasoning was unknown most of the time. He could take on many different forms and sometimes he seemed to even be an indescribable being however- he usually took the form of a dark skinned man.

It is also said he was looking to inflict nothing but pain and misery upon others, but obeyed the will of Azathoth "wholeheartedly". A strange character, I never really seen any people with skin that much darker than mine so I took the account with a grain of salt.

As I read on and on I found about other beings, in other states- but some of them were oddly sparse. Nothing really strange happened until I started to read about the being known is C'thulhu however... part of me wishes I never picked up that book because as soon as I started to read it and go to that chapter that's when things really started to get weird.

Chapter 5

1

Months passed most monotonously that is until I started to read the Necronomicon about C'thulhu.

The first thing I did as soon as I got to the chapter was pronounce the word "Kluu-thoo-lulu?" It didn't seem right, it seemed like a horrible tongue twister and the joke was on me for saying it. But as I continued to read things got stranger and stranger..

I'm not sure but it looked like the book was taking on this weird kind of tone now, it was no longer what it was before.. like someone grabbed it from the author and scratched this entry in here. In some parts it was oddly sparse, like content was meant to be added afterwards only that the author never got around to it.

I want to stress to you that, reading this could be dangerous. I had my own strange experiences that I will get to soon but I feel that I must share some of the dialogue in this chapter in order to really emphasis how odd it truly is. If you wish to avoid any kind of... disturbance in your life, skip ahead now. I know I might be sounding like a tiresome warning from the books which I expressed earlier but I warn you take your time to consider this. I am about to share with you an almost direct word to word writing of this book within these pages.

Chapter 27

C'thulhu

C'thulhu is love.
C'thulhu is justice.
C'thulhu waits in the bottom of the sea
in unending sleep, undying sleep. He who
shares with Azathoth this one aspect of life is
warned.
Oh C'thulhu.

It read like a love poem to this strange
deity as if this person suddenly decided to
throw their whole soul into it. I felt sick while
reading it, something about it churned my
stomach and made me question myself and my
reality. Perhaps it was just a stick joke I don't
know..

He sits at the bottom of the sea
in R'yleh. Waiting.
Waiting for his time of resurrection.
When he will rise from the seas once more to
reclaim the earth.
He whispers into my ear as of now.
Things that shouldn't be known, things that

shouldn't
be explored. The blackness of space and time,
the
whole hopes of whispers from this, undead
God.

> *He which is the priest of the Outer Gods*
will usher in a new state of being when they
return. We will be apart of that, all of us. We
will be in one
with C'thulhu as those who would be one with
him.

> *Ph'agleth! Ph'agleth C'thulhu! C'thulhu*
fthgan syha'h!
> *C-ph'nglui hai. We shall share the will.*
Share the sky. K'yarnak shug!
> *Death awaits us.*
> *Death knows us.*
> *Death*
> *Death does not know C'thulhu.*
> *We must wait for the Lord's child of*
creativity.
> *C'thulhu rise!*

Then there were the spells, hundreds of pages of them related to this one god, I was confused, they looked to be scribbled on in haste as it the person was worried they would forget it if they didn't write it soon enough. But at the end was one quote I didn't quite understand:

"That which is dead eternally lies, but with stranger eons even death may die."

I closed the book and when I did I must've fell to sleep again. I didn't remember falling to sleep though, I didn't even remember going to bed. All I remembered was being bathed in this strange light that seemed to have dark patches in it, and when I woke up I was on the floor half dressed drooling on myself.

It was almost time for my shift too, I was going to be late. I quickly got up and got there just in time before the shift broke. It felt like forever- the corridors were all shifting and turning- I'm not even sure how I made it there in time.

The rest of that day felt like a waking dream. The fear of something watching me was growing, and I was starting to hear odd whispers down the hallway, like the whispers of something beckoning me. I ignored them, but I started to shake more and more the louder they got.

It was similar to that dream I had before, with the blaring noise, but once it got bad enough- it was like it was there but it wasn't there. There was something present but I wasn't sure what it was and it was starting to drive me mad.

"What are you doing?!" The boy across from me asked.

"Huh??"

"You're acting weird stop it! Someone will see!"

I looked around, there was nobody else in the hallway though there were cameras. I didn't know what I was doing or what I wasn't doing. I just tried to stay there but couldn't keep still. It was like there was electricity in my bones or something.

I wiped my mouth and didn't know I was dripping with sweat. How long was I like this. I looked around, it felt as if it was getting darker and darker outside. I swear it was night when I last looked and now things looked different. Everything seemed to be melting. I looked at the boy across from me, he was now a decaying corpse frozen there in front of me, staring forward- one eye still oddly unaffected.

I went up to him and stared, "Hey, *HEY!* Are you awake?" I asked. I went to poke him and my finger went right through the cloth of his uniform and pulled out dust. I squealed and moved back- I could see strange insects start to come out of his body. It looked like he was almost bubbling, full of them-

I ran, and ran as fast as I could- away trying to find someone anyone who could help me. I moved to the end of the hall and turned around. Everything was strange and altered- it was all rotting away- and as I skidded on the ground I could feel a presence- this strange kind of undertone- this blackness that was peering into everything around me and was eating at reality. I fell on the ground- the it smelled like rust and blood- I turned around and looked the glow of the lights that buzzed louder, and louder than anything else I heard before until I heard it- those big stomping foot falls in front of me.

I got up, quick and turned around and then I saw it. This black, thing, a shape of a human body. It's shadow spun out from it's head to this weird wide looking shadow that dance and scampered on the wall with things in it. Human limbs, insect limbs, other things that I can't describe- it looked like a pantomime. Behind it it was tugging something.. It was all dark behind it and the voice whispered to me, they told me to run but I couldn't. I was stuck there.

It drug forward it's other arm- it looked like it was holding this strange long snake- only it wasn't a snake. It was more like a slimy slug, you could see little things squirming inside it's yellow belly- but the top was all black, black like glistening tar.

It flopped and squirmed around on the floor, trying to get itself free, instead the being took it and hit me with it so hard it knocked me against the wall. I could feel the wet slap and the strange residue all over my face. I screamed seeing the tiny little worms and things in my hand. They looked like they were going into my skin.

I slid on the ground, trying to get away, I almost slammed into the wall- I turned around fumbling backward as the figure standing there just let the creature go. It swam quickly through the floor towards me and I ran- ran as fast as I could until I couldn't.

In front of me I swear was this wall of brown crawling insects and things. I turned around and saw the darkness looming. Either way I was fucked. I couldn't get out of this. I was shaking so bad I stared, looking at the small gun in my holster. I almost completely forgot about it.

I turned holding up the gun shaking so badly waiting for the slug thing to come around the corner. I wasn't aware that the floor around me was starting to become so decayed it gave way and broke. Tossing me into the shadows as I fell from such a distance I thought for sure I was going to be dead.

That's when I woke up with such a slap it felt like it broke my jaw. I got up and looked around almost crying.

"W-where am I? W-what happened?" I was still on the ground where I was before, it looked like I never left the area at all.

"You fell asleep!" The commanding officer said.

"I fell, asleep?" I said, I could feel the hot tears coming down my cheeks, "H-how?"

"Because you're a fucking ingrate that's why! Take her to lock up!"

The dragged me into this strange cell, the door was like an iron door to a safe. They just threw me in there with the darkness.

"No! Not the dark! Not the dark!" I screamed as they put me into the void and closed the door.

I panted and looked around the room. I could see nothing. But for a moment I heard a slithering noise, a noise of something dark and slimy in there with me like a snake or some other large kind of creature.

Oh my god! I thought, it's the slug... the slug!!

I paused and hugged my knees close to my chest, shivering and crying at the same time. I didn't see anything, but I heard it, the sounds of whispers.

2

I tried to stay near the door, the only place where a crack of light was still visible and I closed my eyes as I felt the slimy slithers of things creeping up behind me. For a moment I thought for sure I was going to be grabbed and pulled into the darkness but then- I sensed the movement retreating. I sighed, I must be still imaging this, I must be still and focus. Breathe in, and out.

I closed my eyes and tried to pretend I was elsewhere, tried to pretend I was in some kind of glowing meadow but the atmosphere was overpowering, it was too much for my psyche to handle and I was pulled back into the blackness as soon as I opened my eyes, wide.

I continued to stare out, trying to looked through the crack when I heard this strange chorus of pipes, like squeaking and groaning from the ground and almost immediately after a voice came up- it almost bubbled up like from some unknown dark sewer at the very bottom of the this black void.

"You really got yourself into a mess here haven't you..?" The voice said, it sounded deep and mature, almost gravely.

I turned around, and only seen this glowing ember of a cigarette behind me-nothing else was illuminated.

"Who are you?" I managed to whimper, holding my legs closer to my chest.

"Oh, I think you know the answer to that, Runie.." the man said, he cleared his throat.

I stared, trying to figure out if what I was seeing was real or not, the strange numerous colours dancing towards me in the pure blackness.

"What do you want..?"

"I think you know the answer to that too..."

"I don't." I said, furrowing my brow.

"The book. Stop reading it."

I moved my legs away in the blackness, still trying to hold them close to my body- unsure if something else was going to move out and grab me at any moment.

"The Nemonomicom?" I said, mispronouncing it.

"Necronomicon. My god child, how did you get anywhere in this life..?" he sighed, and inhaled from the cigarette again.

"I'm only 11." I said.

"A child, but soon you will be a woman. And if you want to be a woman you will do what I asked. Stop reading the book."

I considered this and grumbled, then said through my teeth "Maybe I don't want to be. What kind of life is this anyway..?"

"A good question. This world has fucked itself so badly, I don't have to do anything. In a way it's kind of a paradise for me. But in another way it's most boring.. The only way to really have fun is to be a hero."

"A hero?" I said, "What kind of person is a hero who murders in cold blood-"

"All heros murder, it's part of the reason why they are called heros. Some people deserve to be killed you know. Surely you realize this, you're exceptionally bright for a 10 year old.

I cocked my head, unsure what he meant.

"You're on a path which you cannot possibly comprehend. You will take this step if you will continue to read the book. But you gotta ask yourself, is this really want you want?"

"I read it because I need something interest.." I said almost whispering.

"You are reading something not meant to be known by most men, let alone little girls. If you keep on reading these nightmares will continue."

"I have to find out the truth!"

"Truth? What is truth but another lie in this world, a lie in a lie in a lie-? That's what your world is. Just another lie, you will never discover the truth because there isn't any. And if you did know, your life would be ended like that. Go back to sleep. And Join Azathoth in eternal slumber.."

I stared as I saw the ember continue to glow and move around in the blackness.

"...how do I bring this to an end..? I want to end it. End all of this.. none of this seems right." I said in a low voice, I could suddenly hear the anger and sadness in it. For a moment the man said nothing.

"KEEP IT QUIET IN THERE!" a voice said outside banging on the door.

I looked away and as soon as I looked back I swear I saw that ember almost right beside my face. I could feel the strange unholy breath of whatever this thing was brushing against my cheeks and I heard the voice coming from this person in here with me.

"You're right.." he said in a strange utterly choking voice.

He moved back to his original seat, no, floated back- and sighed.

"It was nice talking to you Runie. It's nice to talk to people without having them go mad with the rejection of reality hovering around them like a cloud."

"Tell me a way to change it-"

"If you want to change it;" he said, sighing once again, "Be a hero. If not you aren't going to do that, then why not just kill yourself right now?" He said, annoyed.

"We'll be watching.. see you space

cowboy!”

I cocked my eyebrow and looked as the ember flew up into the black darkness of space- flying out into infinity.

I stared and suddenly the door opened with the guard looking at me, I winced looking forward into the blinding light.

“Your time is up!” the guard said.

I stepped out confused, and looked back, almost starting to shake. There was nobody else in there, in face, other than the hole in the middle of the floor, the room was extremely tiny.

“Was someone else-” I began, then stopped.

I got up and tugged on my uniform.

“I hope you learned your lesson now,” another voice said, it was my Commanding officer.

“Yes sir!” I said, hoping that the nightmares stopped for now, then remembering what the dark man in the cell said: *Stop reading the book!*

Was that really what he was saying though.. she got the feeling that there was restraint in his voice.. mixed messages.

Why are you bothering.. you're just hallucinating, another voice in my head said.

Hallucinating from what? I asked myself, the other voice was quiet, no answer.

if you want to be a woman you will do what I asked. Stop reading the book he said.

I rubbed my hand against my mouth, my shift already over- I was heading back to my room. His voice still echoing in my head.

The only way to really have fun is to be a hero.

If you want to change it; be a hero. If not you aren't going to do that, then why not just kill yourself right now?

As soon as I looked up at the ceiling I felt like I was so lost, so confused I wasn't sure what I was gonna do. Then I looked back at the Necronomicon.

"The hell with it." I said, I grabbed the book and continued reading it. I wasn't going to just give in, I was going to fight this thing, fight it until the end. And if I went crazy the hell with it, I will be crazy in this crazy world- I won't be the only one.

3

The weeks went by and I got another assignment, it was pretty simple though. It was me escorting the Colonel around with other guards- my job though basically was to hold his bag and to ensure that whenever he needed something I was there to present it to him.

It was early and cold, we could see our breath as we trudged through the streets of the town, close to exclusion zone border.

Warning signs and razor wire were everywhere. This looked rusted and full of teeth. I didn't notice anymore hallucinations lately, so that was good. However I still felt a bit on edge, the extremely nervousness was still there, just lurking on the edge of the horizon.

The small envoy of us moved through the streets, people were stepping away as if we were oil in water- and we didn't stop until we got to a number of those gathered in the centre of this small walkway. People moved away as soon as the Colonel entered and he looked around with a stern face.

"What is the meaning of this gathering?" He asked.

"Sssir.." one of the peasants came up to him, "Thiss my isss charged with heresy towards our kin!"

The Colonel stared at the man, he was in a barrel and looked like he was beaten with something.. however he was currently out of it. He was almost shoulder deep in what looked to be human waste. His face was smeared with it and it looked as if he was force fed at one point.

"What proof do you have for this accusation?"

The crowd murmured and the man handed him a book that looked to be shredded and well used- the torn and chewed up on the sides of the book.

"What is it?" The Colonel's assistant asked. He read through it quietly and stared.

"Since when can a peasant read, let alone get a hold of such a book?" he asked the man in the barrel. He didn't respond.

The Colonel took the book and slapped him with it, slapped him with so hard the pages started to come out.

I stared and looked at the pages on the ground, they looked extremely familiar. It was the Necronomicon.

"Not going to talk are you? Where's his family?"

"BRING 'EM OUT!" The lurching peasant said, the numbers of ragged people poured out tossing his wife and two children out into the muck.

"So what do you say..?" The Colonel asked, looking at his wife.

"I don't know what you mean, I don't have a clue what that script meant my Lord!!" she said.

He grabbed her mouth tightly, "How pathetic! Is this what you call asking for mercy?! Your family is about to be turned to dust.."

He turned around to the man in the barrel, his eyes were wide and white.

"Well? You either?"

"No, no my lord, please spare my family! They-they're not a part of this. It was I who read the book. Only me!"

"So you admit you own it then?" the Colonel asked moving closer.

"Yes sir..!" the man in the barrel said.

"Then who gave it to you..?"

The man looked around mute, his face was in a grimace. It was hard to say if it was from pain or from something else.

"Oh you won't say will you?" The Colonel said, pulling out his gun and aiming it to his family.

"No, no! Wait!!" The man said pleading with the Colonel, "I'll tell you! I'll tell you everything if you just don't harm my family!"

The Colonel stopped and looked towards the man, "Then I hope you speak quickly, your family's lives depend on it."

"It was-"

Suddenly the bullet rang out- it happened in an instant. The Colonel was covered in blood and the man's face was half gone.

"SNIPER! SNIPER!" One of the guards screamed, I ducked holding my head down. That's when all the shooting began. The guns from the guard's made short work of the shanty town close to us, they shot indiscriminately, even the ones who were in the crowd close to us, blood was flying and bodies were dropping. The bullets flew down out and I was hiding. I just closed my eyes my heart pounding.

Slowly the bullets echoed out, and when I opened my eyes I was surrounded by bodies. I shivered, and for a moment felt actual pure joy.

They were killed?? I thought in my mind, I was certain I was smiling nervously, All killed?? Is it over?

I looked around, I couldn't see the wife and the children, but a few people who have gathered were flopped on the ground. I was there along with the other soldiers but I could hear footsteps approaching me.

"We got them all!" A man said- and then stared.

"Oh wait, what about this one?" Another voice said.

Suddenly I was picked up by the back pack and held up relatively high before dropped on one of the bodies below.

"Ah damn, it's just a kid- just leave it-"

"Leave it?!" One of the men jammed their rifle to my head, my eyes widened. "He could identify us!!"

"He's not even looking at us.."

There was silence as the group of men stopped arguing. "Why not take him with us?"

"Take him, look at that gold badge he wears- if we take him with us then the whole army will come looking for him!!

"BUT!" Another voice said, "This could

be the first real leverage in a war we had in a long time.

I stood, motionless, not sure what to do- should I run away? But if I did I'm sure I'd be captured by the army again. It said one should kill themselves rather than be captured but did I really want to do that?

"You, get up." He nudged me with a rifle and I stood up.

"He's got papers.. get them!" They took the sack off me and someone came up from behind knocking off my helmet. I glanced at it in the mud and it was the last thing I saw before they put this burlap sack over my head.

"Check him for weapons!" Another said, suddenly and came upon me going up and down my legs and my chest trying to ensure I didn't have anything else on me.

"Ah, I got a handgun, and a knife.."

"Holy shit..."

"I know right? These are the weapons they give to children!"

"Come on, let's go.."

I said nothing, just stared below at my feet and kept moving on. I was shaking a bit, but still on sides of what this could mean for me- maybe I could finally be free of the army-? Then another voice said-

What do you mean "free"? Nobody is ever "free" they'll make you fight for their side!

I furrowed my brow as they kept on moving me through the mud.

"Come on, faster, faster!!" the man behind me said, knocking me on the back.

"Hey, take it easy will you?"

"Take it easy?! We're at war here! He might look like a little boy to you but these soldiers are trained to kill us from birth, birth!! Trust me I know!"

"I can't see..." I said.

"Just pick him up then!"

The other man picked me up and hung over his shoulder. The mask didn't drop, yet but really I didn't want it to drop. I didn't want to know my way back to this place. They kept moving faster and faster.

"Come on, move it move it!" Another voice said, they all suddenly gathered into this small structure, I could only guess it was a building but in reality it was a truck. The thing turned over, coughed and loudly started. The engine whined loudly and it felt like we were off.

"Anyone after us yet??"

"Doesn't look like it. It doesn't seem like there are even any people on the streets."

"Ah shit, they're probably all afraid!"

I sat silently just staring at nothing. I was starting to get worried though. They normally don't have support to far behind, and if that were true and they did rescue me- what would happen? I've heard of people dying once they were captured by any enemy side.

The another voice spoke up in me: What if they're saving you for blood? What if all the stories about Amaleks are true and these people really are demons who just want to save you for that?"

I didn't sound like that. They sounded

like they were kind of concerned for me even though they wanted me for my status.

But none of them came, it was long and quiet before I heard any of time stop and talk about anything.

"We're almost here, finally- can't you drive this thing any faster?"

"This piece of shit is going the fastest it can, if I push it too hard it will over heat!"

"Great..."

I'm not sure how long I sat there for, half an hour or so, it was a bit jarring but-

"Alright everyone out!"

I moved to get out, unsure what to do when I was pushed forward into the mucky dirt.

"Come on move your ass!"

"My god, show some fucking decency!!"

"Decency?! Do you think they would show us any of that?!"

"He is just a fucking kid!!"

"Both of you shut up!"

I stood up and mumbled, rubbing my

hands of my coat.

"I'm okay." I said.

"See, he's okay."

"....."

The man beside me picked me up and brought me with him, we were outside- then we were in this strange dark place, it felt like we were going up then down then somewhere- I wasn't sure. By the time they stopped they put me down on a chair and tied me to it.

"You're finally back!" A female voice said, "We were getting so worried, where's Tim's family?"

"Gone." A voice said, "Tim turned traitor so we took him out."

"What?! What do you mean you took him out?"

There was silence, and then I could feel someone walk around me. "Who's this??"

"We don't know, we found him at the town centre with the other soldier's probably an assistant or something.

"He's got a gold badge.. are you crazy?!

They're going to come after us-"

"I don't think so," another voice said, "not yet, soon they will go mad though- then we can us him for leverage."

"Leverage?" She said, then took off my mask.

"What are you doing?!" the man before me asked.

"What does it look like? He's not an animal, are you?" she said looking at me. I just stared at her not sure how to reply, or maybe if I should even say anything.

"My, my! What big blue eyes you have! You're a cute one aren't you??"

I looked away, not sure about what to say about that either.

"They're all demons," the other man said, looking at me.

"You can't be serious..." she said, moving her arms around me. "I won't let you hurt him!"

The other man stared at me, mumbled something and moved off.

"Trisha, we really need to be careful around him. We don't know what he's capable of-"

"He just looks frightened, you're scaring the hell out of him!" Trisha said.

"Who cares?! Let's try to make a plan so we can get what we can from the goddamn Mesos!"

"First I say we find out more about what *he* knows.." the man said pointing to me.

"What do you intend to do Giles, rip his nails out?"

"Why not?!" Giles said. "That's what they'd do to us."

I never heard of that happening but I wouldn't put it past anyone.

"Well, why not start with his name??" the other man said.

"Come on sweetie, tell us your name." Trisha said, rubbing my shoulders a bit. It made me uncomfortable to be touched this much.

"...Runie. Runie Ortix." I said.

"Holy shit..."

“Oh God..”

“Are you General Ortix's son??”

I looked at him then, looked back and fourth across the room, unable to say anything, until I suddenly said: “Daughter.” It felt wrong to admit I was my father's daughter. That sounds really weird to me to say that..

“Daughter?? What do you mean 'daughter'?” Giles asked.

“The military doesn't allow women to serve i it- he's lying! He wants us to go easy on him!!” the other man said.

“Sam, calm down you're losing it.” the calmer man said, then bent down and looked at me at my level.

“Why would the General send his own daughter in at such a young age to fight??” he asked, almost in such a caring tone it made me tear up.

“I don't know..” I said, trying to hold back the tears.

“You don't possibly think we can believe him?” Sam said, glaring down at me.

"What does it matter if she's a girl or not?? We have General Ortix's fucking kid here. We hold all the damn cards!"

"I don't know, something about this seems kinda weird.." The man in charge said.

"What do you mean Adam?" Trisha asked.

"I don't know, probably nothing." Adam got up and walked away, rubbing his head. "Either way we gotta do something.. start thinking of ways to make this letter-"

"The letter? You're still going to do it?" Trisha asked, scared.

"Of course what choice do we have!" Adam said, walking towards the table.

Part Two

The Other Side

Chapter 1

1

"I don't think it's such a good idea..."
One of the parents said looking at me
cautiously. "We don't know how she will react
with the other children."

"Oh come on, she's harmless!" Trisha
said coming from behind me.

"I wouldn't call her exactly 'harmless',"
Adam began, "She probably has killed more
people than any of the kids in there that's for
sure."

"I bet she hasn't killed anyone, isn't that
right Runie..?" She said, looking at me hopeful.

I looked to the side, not saying anything.. not sure if I did or not honestly.

"I think he's right we should just let her be by herself for now, if the Mesos come looking for her they could put the other kids in danger you know.." Giles said, putting away the ammo.

"I know! Why not get her to hang out with Conrad?"

"Conrad Xephos?" Adam began rubbing his head, "I don't think he'd have any interest in baby sitting-"

"Well, she's almost his age, and she's in the army too-"

"We don't even know how hold she is-"

"I'm 11," I said, somewhat annoyed. I was starting to get irritated how people were talking like I wasn't there.

A group of men came into the room holding the satchel I had for the Colonel earlier.

"We looked through this, some information of schedules and things like that, nothing too particularly interesting of note." the other man said, then looked at me, "What were you doing there anyway?"

"I don't know, they don't tell me anything." I replied.

"I have a hard time believing that-" The man began until Adam shook his head.

"I don't think she's lying..." he said. "If she was she'd be a bit more... resistant, to us-"

"Maybe that's part of her mission, get captured and let us get fucked in the end." Giles replied.

"I doubt it. We killed almost everyone there, if we didn't get the drop of them then why did they let themselves get killed? I never seen them behave that way before- And she's part of the Golden Kin- if they let her fall into enemy hands they'd be dead already."

"I'm just saying it's an awful convenient thing.." the man said, giving me a dirty look. I ignored him.

Trisha came up and started to talk to Adam, about something.. I'm not sure their voices were too low. I heard them talk about that Conrad character, or at least mention him- then they all looked back at me as if I just said something.

"I guess we can have Conrad look after her, I'll have to talk to him about it-"

"He's going to say no, I'm telling you now." Giles sighed then shrugged.

2

"No." Conrad said, as he continued to work on his weapon.

"We could really use your help with this.." Adam whispered, "she could be holding sensitive information.."

"Well I'm no baby sitter alright?" He said and grumbled to himself, "Why not get one of the mothers over there looking for a new kid to look after her.

"I am not looking for a baby sitter.." he said, then started to whisper something for the next five minutes. Conrad sighed.

"Fine." he said. "But if she gets to be a

pain in the ass I'm not going to put up with it."

The also added while Adam walked away, "If she tries anything funny I won't go easy on her either-"

"Don't hurt her." Trisha said before looking at me and getting down on a knee.

"Don't worry, he acts tough but he's a pretty good guy. Just uh, be on your best behaviour." she said.

I nodded and said nothing else.

As they walked away leaving me in his care, I just stared at the weapon he was working on. It looked to be similar to the weapons they gave me, but it was somewhat different. I didn't know what it was really called though, they simply said "standard issue" it felt like apparently the government wanted to give us least information about the things we were using as possible.

"Is that weapon broken?" I asked.

"No, just maintenance."

I looked at some of the tools and picked on up, curious. It seemed to be old and worn out, I was wondering how someone could use such a thing until he suddenly grabbed it away from me.

"Don't touch that!" he yelled, putting it back on the table. He held up the small kind saw at me glaring at me. "Don't ever touch any of my things!"

"Okay." I said, then sat down quietly. This was almost as bad as before, I rather be with Trisha, at least she seemed to be much better company.

"Are you just going to sit there moping all day?! Don't you have anything better to do?" Conrad asked.

"No, not really." I said, looking around, "How old are you anyway?"

"I'm 13-" he said, "How old are you, like 8?"

"I'm 11!" I said, grumbling.

"11?? And you're in the army? Since when do they let girls in the army anyway."

"They don't.." I said, looking down at the ground, "At least not according to what I heard, my father forced me into this. All I wanna do is get out- I hate this."

"Is that why you let yourself be captured." .

I didn't say anything at first, I wasn't sure what to say. But then a voice inside me said the hell with it. Who cares about saying too much things or not? It's not like you give a shit anyway. Besides if they wanted to kill you they would've done it long before they brought you back to this place.

"Yes." I said, "I don't care about the government or the army."

"Ah ha! So you do have a brain in your head then!" Conrad said, putting his gun down, "Here I thought you were just a little baby, but now it turns out you're really a spoiled brat!"

"What?!" I asked, standing up. "I'm no brat!"

"Yeah right, you spend all your time in your mansion, then get pissed off when they ask you to serve your country for once." he said holding the screw driver to my face.

I stared at him piercingly, "I don't live in side a mansion, I live in a barn! They don't even let me inside the house!" I said walking away. I was just about had it taking anymore from this guy.

"You live in a barn?! Seriously..?" Conrad laughed loudly so much so everyone else was looking at starting to stare at us. I was starting to feel angry, like that time I stabbed that one kid in the cheek before and I didn't like it. I didn't like it at all.

"Stop laughing at me!" I said glaring back at him.

Conrad just laughed harder, I growled, grabbed one of the sharp tools from the case and threw it at him. It flew inches from his head right into the wall. For a moment I gasped.

"AH!" I said, holding my hands over my mouth.

"Whoa.." Conrad said, looking at the knife before looking at the other people.

"I'm so sorry, I didn't mean that I swear!" I said, almost on the verge of tears now.

“That- that was pretty cool!” He said, taking the knife out of the wall, “And it's not even that sharp! How'd you do that?”

“Uh, I don't know-” I said looking around paranoid. I lost my temper again. I'm so stupid! How could I be so careless? Now I almost hurt someone and it was all my fault.

“You must be a lot stronger than you look!” he said, then tried to do the same thing, the knife didn't stick.

After that it didn't take long for the other kids to actually come and sorta look up to me, though the parents seemed a bit standoffish still against me. They were probably right to be though, everything I touch seems to become poisoned at one point or another.

3

I still felt guilty and ashamed though. Ashamed that I let a bit of angry slip through into the open where everyone could see it. And I almost killed Conrad at the same time. The idea of it, if I wasn't off because of being angered gnawed at me. Even now it haunts me and I can't seem to do anything about it.

However, it didn't take long until I started to fit in more and more with people. I tried to be as helpful as I could but some were still weary of me. I suppose that would only be natural, but part of me hated it. Hated the way my own people treated these others- for what exactly? Simply for reading different books and having different opinions?

Though they did kill their own kind before- that kind of thing didn't settle right with me. It gnawed on the back of my head and I couldn't stop thinking about it. I was away from my own books, and when I started to ask if they had any they seemed somewhat paranoid. I didn't want to exactly admit that I was wearing books by myself in defiance of the government- because if something did happen they might actually end up spilling their guts to everyone else about my own secrets.

"Why did you kill your own people over

a book?" I asked Adam finally one day.

"That is a bit of a complicated question for child as old as you to be asking.

"I am a complicated child." I said smiling slightly.

Adam grunted, then looked back at his work before looking back at me, "It was important due to the fact that the power of the Necronomicon did not fall into the wrong hands."

It already has, I thought about saying, but didn't. Instead I decided to play, somewhat dumb-

"What is the Nemonomicom?" I asked, still having a hard time pronouncing it correctly.

"It's..." he began and stopped looking at me, "Never mind what it is. It's nothing you should have to worry about."

I didn't sigh, but I wanted to. I was annoyed by this question. Here people seemed to treat me differently because I was a child- it was magnified- they didn't just say "don't worry" or "none of your business" they added "because you're a child" to it. I told this to Conrad later.

"They're all like that, adults are full of shit!" he said, throwing pieces of bone from the chicken he was eating on the ground.

"They want to make themselves feel better about themselves more than they really are- just like the Mesos!" he said.

"I was never really treated like this when I was back home- but then again they never really did explain anything to me much when I was.." I said trailing off.

"The only thing they did normally, was beat me." I said rubbing my head still remembering all the times when I was hit.

"Oh?" Conrad said jumping off the ledge, "Did it hurt a lot?"

"Of course it did! I hated it! My father did it all the time!"

"Why didn't you kick his ass??" Conrad said, making some weird fighting moves I never seen before.

"Because, he's.. huge! He's like.. really strong and scary."

"Oh Yeah? Bigger than Adam?" Conrad said.

I nodded. "Yes, much bigger, I'd say he'd be 6'5"!" I was probably incorrect about this. I didn't know too much about height but to me everyone looked huge.

"I bet I could kick his ass!" Conrad said grinning.

"I doubt it, I never seen anyone kick his ass-" I didn't want to think about it. I didn't want to think about what my father might do if he discovered this place. Then I began to think, are they really looking for me? Is he really worried about me at all..? It's been two weeks now and I haven't heard anything.

Although the time here seemed to be kind of nice there was an underlying feeling about it, a sense that I couldn't really put my finger on. It was like, just this underlying sight that couldn't be seen by anything, and I wondered the connection. The connection between this place and the Necronomicon. What did it have to do with any of this place and why were the people so desperate to protect it.

"Are you okay?" Conrad suddenly asked.

"What do you mean?" I was suddenly out of thought and a bit confused.

"You seemed to be thinking about something.."

I paused unsure if I should share my thoughts or anything that was going through my head.

"What can you tell me about the necro-nom-icon?" I asked slowly.

"Huh? That old book? They pass around sometimes?" Conrad asked. "I don't really know anything about it, I tried to read it once but it was too complicated for me. It sounded like a bunch of bullshit!"

I considered this, and he could be kind of right. Maybe I take too much things and face value, maybe I take too much things too wholeheartedly.

"I didn't mind it, but I didn't have much other books to read- okay, it was all wrapped up in a box. With wax around it, I was curious."

"So then, why not tell me what it's about.." Conrad asked sitting back with his legs crossed.

I tried to explain the concepts, the ideas and the things that came through to me with the Necronomicon. The ideas and things conveyed through it were a bit hard to understand, but I think he ended up getting most of it.

"So, it's about a bunch of gods and earth?" he asked when I was done.

"Yeah something about that, how they will all come back one day and claim everything that was taken from them. Kind of beautiful in a way.." I said, glancing to the side.

"You think that's beautiful? They're hideous monsters! That's what the guy who wrote the book said, right?"

"Well yeah-! But, I think they're just misunderstood!" I said.

"Misunderstood? How do you figure that?" Conrad asked.

"Yeah I just feel, like they're misunderstood somehow.." I said, "I guess that doesn't make a lot of sense does it?"

"Haha! Probably because you're a girl! You girls feel sorry for everything!" he said smirking.

I cocked my eyebrow at him, do I really? Is that really what it means to be a woman?

"Is that what really makes me a girl? Just feeling sorry for stuff?"

"That and crying over everything so easily.."

"Hrrm.." I tried to think when the last time it was when I cried. I couldn't really considered it, but it seemed to be almost constant. That I was crying all the time and I didn't even know it. "Maybe you're right.."

"I- Huh?" Conrad said looking confused and surprised, "I- I am?"

"Yeah, maybe!" I said, jumping down.

"I don't know, I haven't been around any other girls at all, I don't think the ones here like me very much.." I said looking a bit disappointed.

"That's cuz everyone thinks you're scary or something. You're pretty harmless! If they knew that I'm sure you'd have lots of friends here."

"Really?" I asked, hopeful.

"Yeah! I mean, I don't see any reason why they wouldn't be. You seem to be pretty nice, a crappy soldier though-"

"Ah haa.." I said, sticking my tongue out a bit, "Well, I think you're right about that. I don't feel like a very good solider, I don't even wanna be one-"

"No one does!" He replied.. then stepped close to me and suddenly, kissed me on the cheek.

I jumped surprised, wondering what the hell he just did.

"Why did you do that?" The last person that did that to me was my Nana, and I didn't understand.

"Uh, should I have not have-"

"No, no wait it's okay!" I asked, "I'm just confused.. that's all.."

"Uh, don't get upset!" Conrad said, "I didn't mean to I'm sorry!"

"No, no! It's fine it's fine! I think.." I said. "Why did you do that?"

"Uh, I guess, you seemed to need it?" he said. But before I knew what was going on he grabbed me and kissed me once again on my lips. For a moment I was kind of in shocked again, but then it felt nice. Until he stuck his tongue in my mouth then it felt really gross.

"EEEEEEEEEEEEEEWWWWW! What was that?!" I asked.

"I-I'm sorry!" Conrad said.

"That was gross! Don't do that again!" I said, grumbling and walking away. Somewhat feeling odd.

"Uh you aren't mad at me are you?" Conrad asked, I said nothing, extremely grossed out. My feelings about him now somewhat changed from before.

I think I'm gonna be sick.. I thought trying to hold myself back from vomiting.

4

It was a few more days until I even saw Conrad again. I spent most of the time in my room and the thought of what happened still majorly grossed me out. He came up to me and looked fairly upset apologizing to me saying he won't do it again.

I said fine, not sure what to do, but he looked like he was about to cry so I forgave him. The last thing I wanted to do was to make anyone cry, especially with something that seemed to be, though extremely WEIRD, incidental.

I told Trisha what happened and she seemed to be oddly delighted.

"OOOh! He kissed you?! That's so cute!! Kind of odd he went so far right away though.." she said with stars in her eyes.

"That was still a kiss? But the tongue!" I said, "Was he trying to make me sick!"

"Don't feel so bad, it's a normal. Just tell him next time you see him you're not ready for that kind of thing yet that's all."

I took her advice, she was pretty good about that. I wanted to ask about the Necronomicon though but that didn't seem like it was possible.

When I finally got to see I did as Trisha suggested, he nodded and looked extremely nervous but didn't want to bring up it anymore. Neither of us did, but that was okay. I was trying to get more information about the book anyway, that's when I started to ask other people about it. Nobody seemed to be willing to talk about it, until that Giles person confronted me and told me to stop snooping around.

"I've already read that.. book-" I said, "I know what is in it, I think I deserve to know the answer-"

"Well you don't, neither of you sprigs do!" Giles said looking at me and Conrad. "So stop snooping around and keep to yourselves!"

He walked away and Conrad did not seem amused.

"That guy has always been an asshole." Conrad said.

"What are we going to do though? We gotta do something to find out what's going on." I said.

Conrad considered this for a moment, then nodded to himself. "I think I have an idea- I think I know where they go to read it-"

"You do?" I asked curiously.

"Yeah, but we can't go now, we gotta wait until night."

5

As I waited for night to come, I fell asleep. I assume night was creeping up, but I didn't know for sure. The room I was in was surrounded by concrete. The bed was still comfier than a hay loaf. There were small pictures of things that seemed pretty normal, a mountain, and a lake. There was a little bookshelf for some of the things I managed to find around here but nothing too interesting. Nothing substantial. Mostly just odd things for children it seemed. Though some of it was funny, I found most of it pretty uninteresting. I was wondering if the books in the mansion were still in their place, then I wondered if they found the Necronomicon in my own possessions. I started to panic, then calmed myself down.

No need to worry about things you can't help right? I said to myself. I mean, nothing you can do while you're down here or anything.

I wanted to keep awake, Conrad said he would come to me when he was sure it was safe to do so. It was so kinda boring in here, and when I read some of the kid books it was starting to give me a headache. I turned around and grumbled deciding to go to sleep, I noticed something on the wall. A strange kind of faded drawing, maybe it was a result of the texture or perhaps someone did put it there but it looked like a face screaming.

That's weird, I thought, getting up, I never seen this here before- and I've been here for three weeks now.

I stopped for the moment as the lights flickered, and for a moment I thought they were going to go out- however instead it steady at a weird, low flow of exposure. Like the light itself was being switched, changed around somehow. That it was being impeded by something.

It was at that moment I started to feel the hairs on my neck stand up- I could feel someone else in the room but I couldn't move. I wanted to turn around but couldn't, that's when I noticed the form behind me, it looked like many tentacles reaching out and licking the air, flickering in the dim light. It appeared for a moment to be this formless mass until it took the shape of a man, then a familiar voice appeared.

"Don't bother to stand, I won't be staying long.." He said..

"W-" I tried to ask but couldn't, my mouth was quivering, then suddenly I could move it freely. "W-why are you here...?"

"I told you not to read the book, didn't I?" He said, "And look what you did, now you're here at the demon's door."

"Demon's door?" I asked. Still staring at the shadows behind me.

"Well, that's what you people may call it. Though the idea of demons and angels are, quite limiting to me."

"Before I came here to warn you to stop reading the book," He began, "Now that you disobeyed that warning- I will warn you again do not go to the ceremony tonight. Or you might very well lose your mind."

"I already lost my mind a long time ago.." I said through gritted teeth.

"Ha! I knew you'd say that, so I will appeal to your other side, don't let your boyfriend take you there, or he will lose his mind too."

"You're just trying to scare me for some reason. That's all you are, that's what you do- you try to manipulate others into doing your work for you- why?"

"You're really too small to see or understand me.." his voice started to deepen as the light started to grow even dimmer. "If I were you I'd be more worried about your pathetic limited existence.."

I furrowed my brow- I was going to say something but then suddenly the light went out and I was thrown into deep blackness.

The darkness swarmed around me, with strange little red eyes appearing in the noise of the darkness itself- it moved around me like a stream and for a moment I felt this other presence again- this other black, evil presence. It wasn't like anything I felt before- it wasn't like a neutral sense, it was evil- fear incarnate. It was trying to make me frightened by the glimmer in it's tiny little eyes.

I closed my eyes again, tight- I could

feel the lights burning into my soul. "GO AWAY!" I yelled- but the sound of my voice just fizzled out like it was in a endless vacuum.

"Hey, Wake up!" Someone was shaking me and I suddenly opened my eyes at Conrad.

"Oh, it's you..!" I said.

"You wouldn't wake up, come on we gotta hurry."

"Ah, wait, is the guard gone?" I asked.

"Yeah, he was there but he's asleep now, so be quiet-!" he told me. I was lucky I didn't yell out from my dream or at least I didn't think I did.

As we slipped out of my room the man guarding it was asleep with his face on the table. It was hard to know it he was truly asleep but if he didn't move I suppose it didn't mattered.

We managed to move through the dark corridors and away from the main open area of the warehouse below, as we went out I could see the sky for the first time in a while, the stars shone brightly but I couldn't really spend any time enjoying the view now- Conrad pulled me along quiet quickly.

I wanted to ask where we were going but I know that was kind of pointless- ahead there were a line of lights from tiny windows that seemed to be relatively tiny- like little squares that were put there for some unknown reason by the designer.

"Right here, here!" Conrad whispered to me, "Get down."

I crouched down and looked through the tiny window where the blaring light came out from it.

It appeared that we were pretty high up, I wasn't sure if they could see us or not but Conrad didn't seem to be too worried. As we watched we could see a group of people in around a half circle as one person in the middle had his hands up and was reading from something. Torches lit around all over and in the middle was a what looked to be a bonfire of some sort.

"What are they doing?" Conrad asked.

"Some kind of ceremony I think.." I
said, trying to hear what they were saying.

"As we begin, let us disrobe and
envelope ourselves in each other! For the beast
of a thousand young demands our own fluids
become one with her during this night!"

They all began to take off their robes
and underneath they were naked, it was hard to
see what they were doing but it looked like they
were kissing each other or something.

"What's happening?" I asked, "Why are
they doing that?"

"I don't know.." Conrad said, "This is
really weird.."

As others chanted and remained clothed,
the mass of bodies below continued to mingle
towards what looked to be one living mass. The
chanting continued: "IA! IA! SHUBB
NIGGURATH! IA IA! SHUBB
NIGGURATH!"

"What language are they even saying?"
Conrad asked.

"I know this, I think... I seen this

somewhere before.." I thought for a moment. "Yes in that book, it's what they call a 'spell'."

"A spell?" Conrad said, "Like a magic spell? For what?"

"I don't know.. I think it's to summon something.."

As the continued the chanting got louder and louder, the fires below getting brighter now as in to response with the chanting until the flames from the bonfire grew so high they almost licked at the ceiling above, where we were. The flames flew up and dripped there, like liquid and it was forming into something.

A strange charred mass started to appear all over the ceiling- taking on strange forms that looked like thorns and tree branches. The branches went wild and spun around like thorns on a thorn bush, soon the ceiling was covered with it- and the flames started to grow dimmer as the trees became blacker and more filled with life. Soon strange heads of odd beasts appeared, they looked like they had many eyes, some looked deformed, all crying out and screaming at each other. The people stopped when they noticed the form was starting to take shape above.

We moved away for a bit, thinking the branches would come close to the window and maybe even break it, but they stopped just short of it.

"Shit..! Wh-what the fuck??" Conrad said, starting to shake.

"Quiet..!" I said, "Something is happening..."

Suddenly the branches and thorns all started to pulsate.. a strange sickening sweet smell filled the air, even from where we were and I wasn't sure how to describe it even now- if anything I'd say it smelled- pubic.

The pulsation came on faster, and faster until a gush of fluid came forward ans spilled all over the ground, suddenly a head came out- a massive jaw that was covered in teeth and looked like it was adorned with wrinkle new flesh of some strange unborn child.

It let out a scream so loud, the windows

started to shake, in fact everything started to shake.

"We gotta get out of here!" Conrad said, starting to panic, "let's go-"

"No! We have to stay! I need to see!" I said, crawling to the window trying to peer through it. The people near the beast were fleeing, some stayed, the man with the book was saying something but we couldn't make it out.

Suddenly the creature turned and opened it's mouth yawning, it vomited something that looked round and dark, like an egg.

"I think I am seriously going to be sick.." Conrad said, turning around and leaning against the wall, he did not look good at all. He looked pale and like he seen a ghost. Not that I could blame him.

"Come on," I finally said, "We better go.."

I took him by the hand and lead him away. He seemed to be unable or unwilling to help me find my way back, but somehow we did. When we got there, the man who was sleeping was gone.

"Okay, we're back," I said, "Can you make it back on your own?"

"I think so," Conrad said, "I feel kinda tired..."

"Don't worry! Just, get back, and remember let's not say anything to anyone- understand? Anything!"

As I went back into my room, I wiped my brow being totally unaware that I was covered in sweat. What the hell was that thing? Was it real? And what was that egg?

Maybe that guy was right... this was a bad idea.

Chapter 2

1

The next day when I seen Conrad he did not look good at all. If I didn't know better I'd say he caught the flu or some kind of other bug, his skin was clammy and pale, he seemed disorientated and somewhat apprehensive, almost paranoid.

"Are you okay?" I asked him, worried.

"Huh? What? Am I??" he asked, unsure of himself.

"You look sick, maybe you should go lie down-"

"No, no I can't!" he said, and started to

pace in my room. "I, I, I can't trust anyone now! They're all in on it I'm sure of it!" he said rubbing his head.

"Calm down! Uh, here, why don't you just lie down on the bed for a bit.." I asked him, he did just that holding his knees to his face.

"I can't get what happened last night out of my head! What were they all doing there, and that thing!!" He said rocking back and fourth, "I'm sure someone saw us!"

"I don't think so," I began, "if they did they'd surely would have confronted us by now.." I said then looked at the door.

"What about that screaming?! I was thinking about it and I am sure someone heard it, somewhere, someone did! What if everyone heard it!"

That was true, that scream was pretty loud... and was right outside. But nobody came out here at all, did they?" I looked around the room and paced a little.

"We should probably leave.." I said suddenly without thinking.

"Huh? Leave? Where are we going to go?! There are mesos all over the place now, looking for you!"

"They are?" I asked.

"Yeah, they wanted to keep it hidden, but the whole idea of having you as a ransom fell through. We were going to send a note but the people with it got captured, we haven't heard from them sense.

"Damnit.." I said, then looked around, "Something tells me we both have to go, if they catch us they'll kill us for sure- or worse!" i said, worried.

"Huh? What makes you think that?"

"Like you said, about last night, there is no way they won't hear that.." I said, walking around, "Maybe you're right, maybe there isn't any place to escape to, but any where is better than here."

"When, when should we leave.."

I thought for a moment, trying to pace this out in my head. If we ran away now, it might look too suspicious.. but if we didn't-

"What about that egg?" Conrad suddenly asked.

That's right too, that egg. That is what it was wasn't it? That thing spat out some kind of round thing covered with thorns.. it was an egg. It had to be. Something like that anyway.

"Ah, my head, hurts.." Conrad grabbed it and I went up to him holding his hands.

"Relax! We'll never get out of here if we don't think of a way through calmly."

"Y-you're right. It's just that since last night I couldn't sleep. And when I try to think through things rationally it's like, something suddenly clouds over it like a dark storm.."

"Something tells me we should leave soon.. We'll go tonight."

"Tonight? How are we going to get passed the guards?" Conrad asked even more nervously.

"Same way as we did last night, I'm sure they're not worried that much about us, now are they?"

Conrad nodded. He still didn't look

good, and as he stood he almost fell over, I barely caught him in time.

"You gotta watch yourself!" I said, "Maybe you should go to the nurse.."

"No, I need, I need to stay alert!" he said, steadying himself on my shoulder. "Who knows what they may give me.."

"They'll give you something if you pass out in the middle of the yard whether you want it or not, so you better go."

He sighed, and gave in in a grumpily like fashion.

"Good, now, if we get separated... where should we meet?"

Conrad tried to think. "I'm not sure... there's an old abandoned store outside across the street, they use to sell telephones or something. There's an secret hatch there attached to the sewer line. We can maybe meet there.. it shouldn't be too hard really to find the way across."

I nodded, "If they come sooner than we expected.. then we may have to." I paused and looked at him, he still looked pale and sweaty. I sighed. I didn't know what to know or feel about him. The whole thing about earlier gave me mixed feelings now and we were in this whole mess. It was my fault.

"This is my fault." I said trying not to look away.

"What? No, I was dragging you there, it was my fault!"

"No, no." I said, and paused walking away, "I got a visitor, last night.. someone came into my room and warned me not to go to the ceremony."

"Huh? Someone did find out?!" He asked, suddenly his skin grew paler than before, "Who?"

"Uhhh.." This is the part which was really hard for me, because I wasn't exactly sure who or what it was.. "I'm not sure. I'm not even sure if I dreamed it or not. But it felt real.."

"So you dreamed this..?"

"I didn't, I had the same experience before and I was awake. It was when I was put into a jail cell for insubordination.." I said. "When I was working at the base."

Conrad looked confused and sat back down on the bed. "Man, I could use a cigarette right about now.." he said.. holding his head. "Just tell me."

"It was dark, he was.. covered in these weird tentacle things. I think it was one of the creatures from that book, the Necronomicon.."

"You think? Why would they come for you, you didn't do anything, did you?"

"I don't think I did.." I said, "But they said they were watching me.. they said that I shouldn't read the book and I shouldn't have gone to that ceremony either. They seem to want to push me away from it for some reason."

"Why would they want to do that..?"

"I don't know!" I said rubbing my face.

"Do you know who it was.."

"If I had the book I could show you, I think.. he was the only one who appeared as a human. He had this long funny name.. Nalyahanna or something like that."

We both stared dumbfounded.

"I never read that thing, so I am unsure.. but maybe we should find out before we leave." Conrad said.

"No, it's okay, I can find out on my own somehow I'm sure of it. There has to be more information.." I responded.

We went over our plan as to what to do and where we should meet up in the end of the night. It seemed to be a solid plan, but I was a bit worried maybe we will end up getting captured anyway. But if we ran into the exclusion zone we should be somewhat safe for a while until we found a way to get out and hide somewhere else. I didn't know how stupid this all sounded though, or maybe how fool hardy it was. But we had to do something. The people here, could no longer be trusted, who knows what they were planning to do and I couldn't let my one and only friend get killed by them.

Conrad said he was going to go to the nurse's office. I agreed it was a good idea, and he actually kissed me again when he did. I didn't object this time but at least he didn't stick his tongue down my throat, so that was something to be thankful for. I just wished probably it was a bit more special- but my feelings about him were still jumbled. I had no idea of how to feel about him at all but in a sense I was grateful he did because I never got a chance to talk to him after that.

When I went to look around to gather some information everything else was blocked off. There were guards everywhere and they seemed to be intent on keeping people from straying out from the large basement area that acted like a village to them for so long. People just gathered there and had there own little huts and things built for them. But none of them seemed to be very interested in defying the guards and without Conrad I couldn't find my way around without him. I had to ask the old fashion way- and there were only two people who I still trusted, Trisha and Adam.

I didn't see either at the ceremony, but they were probably there. They had to be, they were in charge for a certain amount of time. And I had to ask them about what happened last night, they had to like, be around here somewhere and the only place where they could be would be up near the large observatory platform overlooking the village from above. That was the only place they could possibly be, I looked all over everywhere else. But when I did try to go up I was stopped by the guards.

"Where do you think you're going little girl?" One of the guards asked.

"I need to speak to Adam, it's urgent." I said.

"Aw, it's urgent, did you hear that? Isn't that cute?" The other guard said.

"Nobody can see Adam right now, go back to playing with your little dolls or something."

I shook my head and sighed, deciding to head for the kitchen, lucky for me Trisha was there and she did seem preoccupied. I didn't think there would be any other person I could talk to.

"Trisha-" I began- but something weird was about her. She was talking to herself rather quickly, almost in a giddy like fashion. It sounded like gibberish and she had the same look Conrad had. Pale, and clammy. It did not sit well with me.

"GottagetthisrightthistimeifIdon'tI'msure Iwillbeintrouble.." she said under her breath.

"Trisha!" i said a bit louder, "Are you okay?"

"Huh? What?! Oh Runie, I can't play right now I'm busy-" she began.

"I don't want to play, I have to ask you something very important.."

"What is it?" she asked, half listening.

"What was that sound last night-" I began.

"Sound? Huh? What sound I didn't hear

any sound." she said, almost to herself a side note."

"I heard a screaming." I said, "It woke me up-"

"I'm sure you were just having a bad dream. Now I have-"

"Someone was in my room last night." I also stated.

"Huh? Someone was in your room?" she stopped and looked at me, panicked. "What do you mean?"

"Some dark person was in my room last night."

Trisha gritted her teeth. "That perverted fuck!" He took the knife from the counter gnashed it again an onion. "I'm gonna kill him!"

I stepped back afraid, she had this look in her eyes that didn't look exactly human at that point and for a moment I was almost afraid she was going to use it on me. "What? No, no! I mean, there was a man in my room-"

She turned around, her attitude

changing, "Oh honey, I'm sure it was just a bad dream, that's all-"

I didn't like this, she seemed all over the place. Like not really there at one moment, and then the next, sorta there.

"Uh yeah, you're probably right.." I said, then turned around and walked away. I gathered some food from the kitchen. It didn't look like she was even paying attention, and then walked out heading back towards my room to plan more for tonight.

3

I spent the rest of the day in my room. Or wanted to, I couldn't think of anything else to say to anyone else out there. They all seemed to be getting more and more upset by the minute. They had sweaty faces, nervous stares and their eyes- something about it looked like someone got in there and messed up their minds. I wasn't sure what it was, then I thought about Conrad and shivered. What if he is like this too? What if whatever was happening was not reversible?

It's a bit too late to worry about that now, I thought and sighed laying back on my bed looking up at the ceiling. Who was that man? I just couldn't remember his name- I could almost see it written in that book then sighed.

Outside, the world seemed far away but I could hear shouts and what seemed to be rustling somewhere. I didn't pay any attention first, I was still in my own little world, but when I heard gunshots that's when it really got me out of my day dream. I was almost stumbling when I heard the blast and I ducked under neath the bed- unsure what was going on. Did people suddenly start to succumb to their madness, or was it something else? The thoughts were flying through my head and when that door flew open I was sure someone was going to come in and do something horrible- as it turns out I was half right.

The people who did come through were

special ops. They looked to be fully garbed in their uniforms and had their guns drawn.

"*YOU! COME OUT OF THE BED WITH YOUR HANDS UP!*" They screamed.. I slowly squirmed out from the bottom of the bed holding up my hands. As soon as I did, they turned they threw me to the ground and wrapped my head in some kind of dark hood. I couldn't hear anything else beyond the screaming and the bullets flying. I must've been put somewhere out of the way. My only thoughts now though was to hope Conrad wasn't stupid enough to put up a fight and run. But something told me I was wrong about that.

4

I don't know how long I was sitting there for, but my feelings of dread became more and more apparent the longer I sat there. I prayed to whatever god was out there to please like Conrad be okay, please let him be able to escape safely. And soon the lul of the bullets stopped, there was still screaming and crying, but it was distant somewhere- it felt like it was underwater.

I was starting to feel tired from all the excitement that was going on, I was starting to drift off when they suddenly sat me down in what felt like a cold chair. They lifted my mask off and suddenly I couldn't believe what I was seeing. My father was there there in full garb of the black ops unit. He seemed to be irritated as always, but it made me wonder why he was here.

"Father..?" I asked confused, "What are you doing here?"

"What do you think?" He asked grinding his teeth, "I'm here to safe your sorry ass. Honestly, I'm surprised you're still alive." he said as he walked away stretching his hands.

"I thought I could gather some.. information from them if I was-"

"You sure didn't seem to be too interested in escaping though." He said looking back at me, I glanced outside. They were starting to kill prisoners though the window, I tried to ignore it but it still erked me.

"Why didn't you commit suicide?" He asked me peering at me with his steel eyes.

"I didn't think it was necessary."

"Necessary?! You're a soldier! all be it a child, but..." He trailed off, looking outside again as they started to shoot the prisoners in the back of the head. "You were always a shadow of a solider, but a traitor? I didn't think that was possible- even if you were useless."

"I didn't betray anyone!" I said, not sure if that was true or not, but it felt true. And even if it wasn't I didn't owe him or anyone else anything.

"I wish I could believe that.."

Another officer came forward, it was hard to tell what his expression was but he seemed agitated.

"Sir, what should we do with the women and children down stairs?" he asked.

My father turned to him, then looked at me. I tried not to show any interest but my eyes must've been betraying everything else.

"You know the drill, kill anyone under 5 along with the sick ones. The rest can go to processing."

I could feel the vein in my head thumping. I bit down on my lip to try to avoid shouting out "No" but, it wasn't helping too well.

My father seen this, he pulled out his gun and placed it on the table.

"Go ahead, shoot me." He said. "I know you want to, prove yourself." he said. I looked at the gun then looked away at it. It was temping, a bit too temping.

"Either way you're a failure. If you don't shoot me you're a failure at being a solider- if you do you're a traitor."

I jumped for the gun grabbing it. I stared at him, I was going to do it, I was going to kill this son of a bitch!

"I don't need-" I didn't have time to finish my thought. Someone came behind me and hit me with something. I totally blacked out from the sharp pain and confusion. I tried to move my body, tried to force it to move but I couldn't. I was fading away into this place.

5

When I woke up I was staring at the ceiling with a blaring orange light in my eyes. Everything around my looked rusted and old. I tried to move and couldn't, my hands and feet were both bound and there was some kind of cage over my face.

I tried to free myself, but couldn't. It was tied tight. For a moment I began to scream and then realized I couldn't stop. What was going on? Is this the end basically of me? I didn't want to die like this. Not in whatever this place was- but it was hard for me to do anything about it now.

Then I was moving, someone had a hold of my stretcher and was moving me out some here, into what looked to be an elevator.

"Stop your yelling." The man appeared,

256

he looked to be totally in an overcoat with his face covered.

"Where am I?" I asked.

"You'll find out soon enough."

As the elevator creaked up it moved slowly into a place that seemed to be much brighter. It felt that the place had been cleaned up quite a bit compared to where I was before.

"Doctor, she's awake."

Another man, much older came over and seemed to examine me. He did not look familiar.

"Hm. I see. Well put her in her room. Try to do something about that bruise on the side of her face- I think we can take off the restraint cage."

The man nodded, and rolled me down the hallway. From where I was I could hear more crying. There was always someone crying near me it seemed. No matter where I went there was always someone close by.

The room they rolled me into next was a quiet single room. There was nobody else in it but it seemed neat and clean from the ceiling. The man slowly began to remove the cage around my mouth as I tried to get up and look around.

"Can you remove the-" but before I could as he was gone. I wondered how long I was going to stay here until two other muscular men came to move me from the stretcher to the bed.

"Can you untie me?" I asked them.

"Not until the doctor has cleared it.." the men said.

"What am I suppose to do if I have to go to the bathroom??" I asked, worried.

"You're wearing a diaper aren't you? Heh, make use of it."

I stared in disbelief at this. I was not going to use a diaper.

"I'm not some kind of animal! I demand to use the washroom! I'm a golden kin.. you know.." I said, one of the few times I remember that I actually enacted by power.

"Not anymore you aren't, you're a traitor

here." The orderly said, closing the door.

They were right though. I was a traitor. I hated this place let alone I would never die for it. That's the one thing I promised myself. And now look at me, back at the start were I use to be.

I must've sat there for two hours. Luckily I didn't have to use the bathroom yet but the boredom was getting to me. I must've fell asleep again because when I opened my eyes next the doctor was there staring at me with this strange kind of smile I could only describe as being warm.

"Hello Ms. Ortix, we met earlier but I have to say it's nice to get a chance to meet you face to face in a more close fashion."

I didn't say anything but looked the board as he was writing down something.

"So tell me, do you know why you are here?" he asked finally.

"Because I am a traitor?" I asked.

"That's part of it yes. The other part is because you have been brainwashed to believe you are a traitor. We need to reverse those ideas in your head, try to flush them out."

"Is that why you won't let me go to the bathroom?"

He snickered to himself, "Oh my. Well it is a type of control mechanism we use. However, if I see you are not a threat I will be sure you can be able to go there yourself."

"So, tell me, what was the last thing you remember?" he asked.

I thought for a moment, and wasn't sure. It was all grey and hazy for me. I tried to focus but, I think I was going for a gun or something.

"I was going for a gun.." I said, "I think."

"Yes, yes you were. Do you remember what happened next?"

"No, not really." I said.

"Someone hit you on the head and they restrained you.."

I tried to remember that but couldn't, I shook my head in response.

"Well, either way it doesn't matter. Here

we will try to assess everything you had witnessed from the beginning to end when you were captured.”

“Right now?” I asked.

“Yes.”

I told him the story, but kept Conrad out of it. I didn't want any of them to know I was anywhere close to him or anything. I was sure if I was and he was captured they'd kill him for certain. I didn't really want to know his fate. Part of me still wished he was out there roaming around freely, even if he was somewhat worried about my own situation.

I didn't tell him about the Necronomicon either, or the whole thing with the summoning and that strange creature. I thought it might give them ideas, information they may not need.

“So the last thing you remember was being in your room when the retrieval operation started...?” he asked, continuing to write things down.

“Yes, that's all I know..”

"Hm." the doctor didn't say anything else. He just stared at his board as if he was waiting for time to run out or something.

"So, can I go now..?" I asked.

"Not quite yet, we need to verify these findings.."

"Verify them? How?"

The doctor didn't say, he got up and looked back at me. "Oh don't worry about that. I'll see to it we'll get the bottom of this I assure you."

Bottom of what? I asked. Or wanted to, before I could he left.

"Uh, what about these restraints? Please, can you loosen them??"

I didn't hear back from him. I just sat staring at the ceiling wondering exactly when I will be able to be free. But the whole idea felt futile to me, so I decided to try to think of something else. Something that might cheer me up. Then I started to think of that book I read a while ago, Arabian Nights- that seemed to help an awful lot.

As the sun rolled around the room a man came to me with what looked to be soup. I'm not sure what was in it but it tasted pasty and bland. He fed it to me- or should I say almost shoved it down my throat.

I told him I had to go to the bathroom. He sighed and decided to loosen my restraints and escorted me there which seemed to be one large bathroom with several toilets and tubs around.

"Here use it-" he said pointing to a toilet.

"But I can't go with you looking at me! Or hearing me-"

"I can turn away but I can't plug my ears, so it's either this or using the diaper."

I sighed, went to do my business and when I was finished he turned around, grabbing me firmly and taking me back to my room where he strapped me to the bed again.

"If you behave, you'll be able to roam free." He said as he re-did it.

"Can you, give me something to pass

the time..?" I asked, the man said nothing after leaving, just closing the door and letting me stay there to stare at the ceiling once again.

When night came the shadows had a weird way of dancing around in strange in human shapes. I tried to get my mind off of it, but I wasn't sleepy. In fact I was wide awake. I slept most of the day away and no way interested in falling back asleep. The shadows and the dark room made my imagination go wild.

I sighed and tried to close my eyes to imagine myself somewhere else. It was hard to believe after all this time but I was still a child. And this place was making me free extremely lonely and uncomfortable, more so than usual.

I didn't feel this alone in a while, since I had been separated from my Nana, that was a hard night. This was just long and boring now. However my imagination was insisting there was something in the corner of the room, watching me again. Probably that thing with the red eyes.. I didn't know what it was- and there

was no mention of it in the Necronomicon- or if
there was it wasn't made apparent to me yet. I
didn't get to read all of it completely.. but
maybe there was something I didn't go over
right or correctly. Or maybe...

Maybe that thing with the red eyes was
really just that smoking man from before.
Maybe he's trying to trick me somehow.. if only
I could remember his name, damnit.

But it was impossible. There was no
way to remember his name, not without the
book. And if I told anyone about the thing with
the red eyes I was going to end up staying here
for a lot longer than I wanted, that's for sure.
There was no real way out of this.. until I told
them what they wanted to know I was stuck.

7

I was woken up fairly early in the
morning, force fed dry toast with some kind of
substance on it- it tasted like some kind of jam
but I am not exactly sure what. Then I was

forced to take part in an aggressive brushing campaign of my teeth. They used some kind of machine on it that made my mouth all foamy and soapy. Then they took me to a room with a bunch of other women and all sprayed us off like cattle or something with a large length of hose. That was our bath- I didn't really want to go through with that again but it didn't seem to be much of a choice. Nothing here was.

From then I was wheeled to this kind of, activity room, I'm not sure.. it had a TV there with all sorts of programs but it was mostly on political things of that nature- and some kind of weird patriotic drama. I never seen this before so I found it interesting. My father either didn't have a TV or hid it well in his house, if there was one I am sure I would've found it when I was younger.

However, the dramas were dry they were better than nothing. I was sat there with about 8 other ladies who's names were never revealed to me except for one who I was usually sat beside. She was an older lady, about

20 years old.

"What are you in here for..?" she asked, surprised.

"I'm told I am a traitor, what about you?" I asked.

"The same.."

I looked around, "Is there anything we can really do here or are we forced to sit here all day...?" I asked her.

"Well, usually they give us puzzles or these kind of weird games to find words in.. that's before classes begin. Once classes are finished we-"

"Classes?" I asked, disappointed.

"Oh, you don't care for school?" she asked.

"No, I do not. I hate school. I hate all forms of it, it's terrible just terrible..!" My thoughts suddenly went back to school, all of those training and deplorable killings and torture. It just rubbed me the wrong way.

"Well, it's not really like that, it's more... re-education- OH! By the way I'm Ruth.. and you are?"

"My name is Runie.."

Suddenly a guard came up, "Okay you yente, all of you shut up. We've got a new member joining us here, so why don't you tell us the prison rules No. 8563."

"No Talking! No Running! Do what the guards tell you! Do not disobey! Do Not hide food! Do your absolute best!"

"That's enough." He said bored. "Anyone caught breaking these laws may face punishment which may include execution."

Another guard came around, passing what looked to be books to me and the others. They were red and seemingly blank. These were to be our "work books"

"As you may know you dykes are all a part of our great nation's elite. But you now you don't deserve to be elite anymore, you must earn it again to prove you believe in our cause. Do that and you may leave." He said, before taking out a cigar and lighting it.

"More than half the people who take my

class do leave and go back to their ordinary life.. whatever that may be. But piss me off, and I'll hang you up there on the gallows by your tits, understand? You're all you are to me now is pig shit. That's about it. Now start reading 2049, first page 42!"

The room was quiet.. nobody was doing anything. Was he talking to me?

"2049...? What are you waiting for..?"

I looked around nervous. I didn't say anything.

"For fuck sakes 2049!!" He came right up to my face almost like lightning and smashed his club against the table. "WAKE UP! Don't you know your prison number?!"

"I-I-I-I don't know sir! N-n-nobody told me!" I said.

He smacked his head and grumbled. "You, are Prisoner 2049, now read! You Can read can't you??"

"Y-yes sir!"

"Then stop acting like a stupid twat and read it!"

I looked at the book shaking and began to read.

"From the great awakening we strive fourth to become the best and the greatest country of them all. No country can be greater than us for we are the mountain of the earth and will tear those who dare oppose us asunder! The life we give is nothing compared to the life they give for us, so say it our Country, our Lives, our freedom."

"That's what I'm talking about.. you people need to realize that. You need to realize you are *NOTHING* without this country. You're just insects scurrying around-"

It went on like this every day. Every day they would drag us in here to read from these books. Apparently from what I read, we invented everything. Cars, telephones, radios, television, boats, guns, modern warfare- we were the leaders of it all, and nobody could stand in front of us. Not the country of Judah, or the Kingdom Of Israel.

Those were the only two countries really

mentioned. I wasn't under the impression there were any others. And tests were hard. We had to get 100% or we'd get beaten. Luckily, it really wasn't that hard to get 100% when you read between the lines. All you had to do was answer that the country did it all. But this was a small part of our lives. Of my life.

The next part of the day was really devoted to interview time. They asked the same questions over and over again, asking me if I was an agent of Israel, an agent of Judah. Was I a terrorist, what was I doing with them, what I knew about their movements, etc.

"Now, you know I could do all sorts of things to you to make sure you answer correctly." the guard said, "I could pull your finger nails out from your hands or pull teeth from your mouth. You're not going to get married, nobody will care about that. As long as you're alive we can do anything we can as long as it doesn't leave a scar.." he said looking at the book.

I nodded in agreement.

"So if you lie, and we know you're lying.. you will be punished. We can see into your head you know, I can see that just by looking at you how much of a piece of shit you are you know. I know you're hiding something from me. When I find out you're lying you're going to be sitting with a stick up your ass in that field for hours.." he said pointing outside.

"Don't think you're not the first to come in here, at your age or status either. I'm part of the golden kin circle as well, I know it. It's my job.."

"What if I-"

"*DON'T* Fucking interrupt me you whore, I am fucking talking here.." The man said, he seemed to be almost mumbling and devoid of energy. Like he was just about to fall asleep, but as soon as he snapped at me he was alive again and it just started to rub me the wrong way.

Afterwards, we were all ushered out to do farming. Mostly just pick or plant strawberries.

"...and if we catch any one of you eating those berries we will break every finger in those dainty little hands you have. Don't forget that ladies.." One of the guards said, spitting on of the women there.

I was hungry, but I had no desire to be tortured. At least not yet anyway. It seemed to me there was no guesses to be made on whether or not they'd do it. In fact they almost seemed eager.

Sometimes they would just pick the strawberries out in front of us and act like they were eating the best things in the world, other times they would beat us out of boredom. I was pretty use to that by now but the other women didn't seem to be use to it at all, they would cower over easily crying to the point it was almost embarrassing for them. I wondered just how good they got it before coming here. In fact I was wondering what the hell got them here in the first place.

It didn't last long though, it couldn't. The day was almost out and as soon as night came

they all locked us back into our rooms.
Awaiting the distant movement of the shadows..
I wondered how long was I going to be in here..
how many weeks or months..

Chapter 3

1

As time passed on I came to the realization that it was a lot easier just to agree with what was being told and asked for me than it was to continue to push against it. However, spending time with women so much also made me develop this distaste for men, I started to believe that everything negative happening to me was due to the fact that men were behind it all. They ran the country, they ran the military, and women seemed to be a lot more meek, a lot more measured in response.

Most of the time my experience was somewhat one-sided though, I was always on the other side of the fence- I never really had much of a chance to really socialize with anyone let alone women and it was a nice change of pace. Although most of it was done in hushed whispers.

One day they took us to the other side of the valley. The valley was far but it was surrounded by mountains, it was much too large to be an actual prison camp just for the higher class. Several miles down the road was one devoted to the lower class- it wasn't nearly as picturesque.

The whole area was scrapped up and clear cut. It was meant to help keep our camp and the other resort across from it in comfort. It was small, however there was no denying it. Compared to where we were this place was hell on earth.

Most of the time the the road was just filled with mud, it was so dirty there that you needed boots to go everyplace. The long houses were they jammed people in smelled like putrid rot and sewage. People were separated by sex, except for children- and I was surprised to see children there, mostly running around with no clothing playing in the mud and the dirt and god knows what.

"Ladies..." Our handler said, "This is where you will be going if you end up in our curiosity again- and you won't be coming back out."

The whole place had this grey kinda feeling to it. We were forced to tour this place, and although it was informative there were more than one occasion that I had to hold myself back from throwing up. Sometimes corpses just dotted around here and there, one person was dying on gangrene and the soldiers were just kicking them around playing with them as they cried on the street. It made me both angry and disgusted and wanted to change the system somehow- but I had no idea how to even act on something like that.

When they took us to the killing floor

that's when we mostly lost it. Everyone was in shock- this was suppose to be a secret wasn't it? Except it wasn't. The corpses and people who are dying were "processed" into feed for the prisoners there and god knows what else. They simply took them and shoved them into what looked to be a giant blender. It must've stood two stories high, it looked to be rusting slowly to death. The smell was horrible and flies buzzed everywhere in a frenzy- they were some places where it was so clouded that there were people just covered in black, swarms of moving mass and that's when I was sick.

Vomit almost squirted out from my mouth I couldn't hold back any longer, and I just threw up on the floor. Most of the other soldiers laughed but the other women couldn't do anything to help me. They knew if they did they'd probably end up getting kicked or punched.

"MMMM! Ain't that look good..!" One of the men said.

"I think I'm getting hungry!"

I didn't want to stay here anymore, I wanted to leave badly. The sounds and the high pitch whining of the blender- the flies. Everything. The pulsation of the maggots in the bodies and how they flew and screamed as they were torn apart. It was all some kind of cursed nightmare and I wanted out. Only I wasn't waking up this time. There was no unspeakable black things that lurked in the shadows, or red eyes staring out from me through the blackness. This place was all too much.

They made us sleep there that night. The sounds of people crying and screaming echoed down the halls, the smell and the flies buzzing around also did something to my head- I felt like I was coming down with a fever.

"Why are they making us stay here..?" I asked Ruth as I stared up at the ceiling.

"They want to put the fear of god into us. You heard what that nut said earlier. If we come here again they'll send us here."

"Do you think, they'd actually do that?" I asked turning around.

"Yes, they're crazy enough to. Everyone here is fucking crazy! Everyone- if people knew the truth what was going on nobody would stand for it, no one."

But part of me thought and did think they did know what was going on. Everyone knew what was going on, that's why they showed it to us. Everyone was aware. Was the "outside" aware? Maybe, maybe not. I didn't know anything about the outside of this place.. maybe they would all join together and fight to help to release these people. But who knew why they were really here.. maybe some of the deserved it. However, then again who deserved this?

I just wanted to go "home", wherever home was. Then it occurred to me I didn't really have a home did I? Was home that place with the basement and the books.. it was comfortable.. but so were the barracks and times.

But even then it wasn't home. I didn't have any family or friends. These people could be my friends couldn't they? But were they really? Wasn't it all just a method of convenience?? I suppose I was someone to take care of, someone to watch out for.. but I wasn't an equal to them. I was an equal to no one, not anyone, not anywhere. And that idea made me feel all the more lonelier.

The next day they made us wander around aimlessly, I didn't want to. I just wanted to get away, but they really stretched it out. We didn't leave until about 5pm, and when we did I was grateful to wash and get the smell off me, to get the flies out of my hair and the smell out from my nose. Now all there was was clean air and the smell of the dew from the valley. The prison camp seemed miles away, and I should've felt ashamed but didn't. I felt thankful I didn't have to go back again to it, and it still haunted me.

"Don't come back or you're going to be sent here.." I shivered, I couldn't go to that place again I couldn't. I never felt more ashamed.

I spent nearly a year in there. When I came in as a child, and when I left I was just as confused as to who I really was. I thought I was a woman, but I wasn't really. But it was no denying it anymore, it couldn't be hidden, I was turning into a woman and part of me hated it now that I left my friends behind. My chest hurt, my body hurt, everything hurt. I always felt hungry it was never enough and the damned mensuration was also irritating. Though, later I would find I could get out of things pretty easily by using it as an excuse.

When I seen my father again he groaned at me, he wasn't too excited to see me in my progression. He seemed to be in fact dreading it.

"I see you've changed somewhat." He said distastefully the first time he saw me leave the prison.

I didn't say anything, I just tried to stay

at attention. Try not to whine, try not to complain. Just agree with what is being said and done and use it.

"Maybe we can make some arrangements.." he asked, then sat quiet in the jeep. I didn't do anything but look straight ahead. I could feel he didn't want to be there with me, but he had to make his final judgment. He didn't say anything about refusing me, nor did he object for me joining him so I assumed I was safe. But I learned to always be on the defensive when it came to him.

I didn't know what he was planning but I knew what he could do was somewhat limited, due to the *Concordat of Tsade*. The concordat had many rules, and one stated that no scars should be laid wilfully on a woman. It seemed that these rules were unbreakable for some reason, and why, I didn't know. But they kin circle took them fairly seriously as rules of the caste so, I doubted they could surgically alter me in anyway. If they wanted to they would've done it by now.

As we finally arrived to the airport again, I started to wonder if I was going to be headed by "home" or to the barracks. It seemed like I would still be unwelcome back home either way and after getting so use to sleeping in a bed I was a bit discouraged to find that I had to go back to the hay loaf.

I shuddered to think of going back to the prison camp though. The whole idea didn't sit well with me, and I was still having nightmares about it.

I was surprised when we finally reached the base only to find the things I had brought before all in a box. Who put them there? I was nervous, nervous as I could be, and started to wonder if the book would still be in there. To my astonishment it was gone.. but where the hell did it go? They must've taken it for evidence. Maybe that's why I was sent to the re-education centre or where ever.

I decided not to ask about it, or ask for it. I wondered how Conrad was doing.. and if he was also okay. I wondered if Ruth was going to be alright to or if she'd ever be released from that place. I never really found out why she was sent there did I?

I suddenly felt tears come down my face, so many people I've met, and I still don't know anything about them, how they are or where they're going. Or let alone where I am going. I still felt alone, but at least I had a bed. At least I was out from that place. I had to move forward. For them and everyone, I couldn't stay here sitting and crying about the past- I had to continue.

I closed the box and sat on the bed. I didn't feel any different, I just did what I was told now. And I wondered I started to feel as if something was watching me again. And then that whisper started... something was in here- but it was gone and it was gone in an instant.

3

The next day I was summoned for reassignment. Much to my surprise it was with the armour force.

"We're going about for some plans for invasion, therefore we believe due to your aptitude tests and what not provided, you would do better in our armour division."

The colonel in charge passed me a file with the majority of information on it.

"This says that I'm suppose to be responsible for loading and maintenance of equipment related to armour rounds. I uh, never heard of this before."

"Of course you will be trained for this new assignment. However we'll be expecting it to be finished in no less than a week."

A week? I thought, that didn't give me very much time at all.

"This is an invasion.. where are we invading?"

"That's on a need to know basis," Another Colonel said, leaning into the mic, "When you need to know we will inform you."

I suppose I shouldn't be too shocked, the idea of them giving too much information wasn't really something that needed to be explained.

This time however I left the books of mine at home, I didn't want to risk losing anymore in case I was captured. I was never really given very much training in what to do if I was captured.. which surprised me when they delivered a strange item to me in my mailbox.

"What's this?" I looked at the small piece of paper saying there was something for me to pick up at the armour depot. I was wondering what it could be since most of the "armour" I was suppose to be in charge of was going to be tanks.

When I arrived the place looked messy, but busy. There were many people around trying to get as many tanks replaced and repaired before the mission was suppose to be taken out. Many men stopped and gawked at me, the number of people who did was starting to make me uncomfortable, I didn't think I drew that much attention, however, in retrospect I must admit it's mighty strange to see a woman in a place that was only housed by men. At the time though, I didn't think or believe this- I thought it was something more sexual. Then again maybe I was right to think this. I don't know, but it was probably a mix of the two.

"I'm Private Runie Ortix," I began to introduce myself to the sectary there, "I am here to pick up a piece of equipment."

The man, who seemed more bored of his job than anything else took the piece of paper and examined it, then went to the back to receive the package.

"I'm guessing you probably seen this before so hopefully I won't have to explain it to you.." he came and placed it on the table. It was a long box that felt somewhat heavy.

"I'm not exactly sure.." I stared at it and opened it. When I did I wasn't sure what I was seeing in it. It looked like some kind of strange... sorta what? A belt?

"What am I suppose to do with this..?" I asked confused.

The man sighed, he looked extremely

agitated like I just asked him to do something completely out of line with his regular work schedule.

"It is an anti-rape device." he said, looking at me, I didn't understand still, and shrugged before he continued. "It's a chastity belt."

"A chastity belt? Am I suppose to wear it?"

"Fine, since you seem to be so stupid you don't understand what the hell a chastity device is.." He picked up the belt and held it up. "You wear this instead of underwear, you place it next to the skin. It's to prevent you from being raped or sexually assaulted."

I still wasn't sure what he meant but I nodded kinda.

"So I just take it off when I go to the bathroom-"

"No, you don't take it off. You keep it on for the duration of your mission. You're not even suppose to take the key with you you leave it here."

I shrunk, this thing wasn't light, it was heavy. Not to mention the idea of wearing something like this.. what the hell was the point? I didn't know anything about sex, much less rape. I sighed and nodded.

"Okay, thank you.." I placed it in the box. When I got back to my dorm I tried it on. It was heavy, cold and tight. It was clearly visible when I put my pants over it. I already started to hate it, and didn't see much of a point in keeping it or using it. But since they seemed so intend on it I didn't figure I had much of a choice.

Much to my surprise though, the benefit of this thing would earn me a lot of calm when I finally figured out what it was for. I still didn't like wearing it though.

4

The training did seem rather intense at first, mostly going into the tank, and out of it, running around it, it all seemed to be mostly escape manoeuvres. I didn't meet any of my squad yet, but the people they teamed me up with didn't seem to be that interested in talking and more interested in actually blowing things up. My job as a loader was relatively simple. Just load the rounds into the main guns of the tank, make sure they're kept clean and safe from any outside 'influence'.

The guns were first practice outside, that was easy enough- but the cramped space of the tank made things a bit harder. Lucky for me I was still pretty short and small, the rounds however though compact were pretty heavy. They must've weighed 20 pounds- of course the size and the weight of them in my tiny hands didn't help make things easier. Nobody gave me a rough time because of my caste, which I was thankful for. For a bit I even wore that god awful belt, that made things a bit harder too. I was a lot slower than I would've liked, and the weight of the rounds combined with the weight of the belt didn't make things any easier.

The tank itself, I admit, I kind of liked. I

liked the idea of it, that is how fast it was, and the sound it made of the clink clink clinking of the treads. The thing could run usually fast despite the weight of it- some of them even slid on the ground as they ran their courses. It was kind of fun- but something told me once I got to the real battlefield it would be less than exciting though they tried to make it as real as they could, they even fired real rounds.

Half way through the week, though I was exhausted at this point from doing simple runs around the tank I was introduced to the rest of the crew.

There were four of us (Me included of course), Captain Televana Xellexie, Lieutenant Robert Delasanto, and Cobort Zastarif. They're names were so complicated to me, I just referred to them as rank. The Captain was part of the golden caste, the other two were grey ghosts.

"Hm, you're a little small for a loader, are you sure you can pull your own weight?"

"I will do my best, sir!" I said saluting

him.

"I heard about you, about all of you, I expect the best from all the people under my command, come on I'll show you the tank we will be using."

I was in awe at the size of this thing, it looked to be as big as a house. But of course it was on the smaller side compared to most tanks, if it was any larger I probably wouldn't be able to lift the rounds in it.

As I was told it was an AR-1001, it's top speed was about 50 km/h, it had two kinds of guns, one was a Vulcan cannon as used by the gunner, the thing looked to be a chain gun of some kind. It was large but armoured and seemed to be able to cause enough damage by itself let alone the cannon on it.

The turret itself was sloped with low angles, the gun wasn't too large in terms of rounds but the good news is that it had what was known as an "auto loader", which automatically pumped new rounds into the cannon. The bad news is it had to be loaded with five rounds before it could be used again, that's where I came in unfortunately for me- It was easy for me to simply put the rounds into the chamber by myself, but five at a time? I was more than a little nervous.

The size of the round was about 7.5 cm, but oddly enough they seemed to be pretty light compared to the rounds they gave us during practice. I would say about 5 pounds each. Something in them apparently gave them more explosive power that is what I was told when I asked about them. The rounds just barely fit in my tiny hands and I was barely able to get them into the loader as I trained. I was lucky enough to impress the captain and my other team mates. I was worried that I wouldn't even be able to lift these things since I was sure the real thing would weigh so much more.

As I read the manual for the tank it was quite interesting. Apparently this thing had 1000 horsepower, which made me wonder what it would be like to have this thing pulled by 1000 horses. The rounds came in from armour piercing, to regular rounds to something called Black X rounds. I tried to look up what Black X was, but the information given to me was somewhat limited. It made me wonder why they were so hush about it- we never used Black X in any of our training exercises and I didn't hear the captain mention it at all.

I tried to find more information on Black X, but nobody would give any, either they didn't know or didn't want to know. I even asked the Captain and he simply said it was a "secret weapon" and not to worry about it. But I was worried.

There were only five rounds of Black X out of the 120 rounds that were available. That was an insane amount for something so small.

As the days went on the end of the week came closer and closer to the date of our deployment and they still didn't give any real information regarding this. I started to feel this strange kind of pressure coming out from my other team mates, like they were all on edge. It didn't do any good to calm my nerves, I wanted to ask what was going on but couldn't. I knew if I did they'd probably snap at me and it would be useless so I kept my mouth shut.

I was able to make it through to the end of the week but that's when they told us to get everything checked and maintained on the tank. The whole thing took a while and all along I was thinking "this isn't what I was hired to do was I?" But I kept quiet. And as we started to get ready to go and loaded the tanks into the planes I started to wonder where we were going and why- what the whole point of this all was- we still weren't told anything. At least I wasn't. And I was feeling more than a little conflicted about it.

5

The day we left I wasn't sure where we were going or why. There was no explanation for our mission at all- we didn't get any briefing or debriefing on what exactly our mission was. Or at least I wasn't told about it.

We waited inside the huge plane that carried the armour across the water, I was starting to get more than a little bored but I decided to get some sleep while I was at it. Who knows how much or little I would end up getting at the end of it- that's when Captain Xellexie came along and woke me up.

"Come on, mission briefing is going to start!" he said, "I want all of you to pay attention too they're not going to be explaining this twice."

I got up, finally we were going to find what this was all about, I didn't like to argue or do anything to stir the pot but it was starting to rub me the entirely wrong way how this all was handled. If this is how missions generally are I'm going to be having a really hard time with adapting.

As we did gather for the meeting, it didn't look like people were too interested. They were mostly grey ghosts and grey ghosts didn't really seem to care about anything other than killing half the time. This was my experience..

"We will be attacking the Maltaese strongholds here, here and here. We have been told they have armour as well, but they should be nothing compared to our capability. When and if our targets have been eliminated we will take care of any other civilians and soldier by using Black X. Of course if you're still around by the time it is deployed, that's your sorry ass that's out- not our problem."

I wanted to raise my hand but couldn't, I might end up drawing attention to myself more than I wanted.

"You will all be receiving your assignments by your captains. If you have any questions I suggest you ask them."

We gathered around the captain as he looked at the orders.

"Okay.. we'll be leaving in about 20 minutes, get ready.."

"Uh, excuse me sir," I began-

"What is it now private?" he asked.

"Exactly what is our objective?"

"Why is that important to you? Your objective is to ensure we always have ammo in the loader. That's what you have to worry about. Let us worry about the details."

I nodded. I didn't want to push it.

Alright everyone, let's get ready..

As for tradition, many people write things on the tank to try to either promote themselves of scare the enemy. When they gave me the spray paint to write something on the side I thought for a moment, I wasn't sure what exactly to write. Until suddenly a phrase just popped into my head.

"It figures, a woman would write something like that." Delasanto said.

"Ah, you just made our tank wimpy.." another Zastarif.

"Well I prefer if it said "Kill all Maltaese!" but, I suppose we're stuck with "Hope for All".

I didn't say anything, I was rather proud of myself for coming up with that phrase so I decided not to push it. That's the new me, don't argue with anyone or anything just keep on going through with orders! Don't rock the boat! You don't want to cause any trouble. Deep down I hated myself.

We all go ready, what I didn't know about getting ready is.. that the tanks were all dropping from the air. I didn't know that was possible, I think they'd be destroyed for sure if they simply left the aircraft considering how massive they were. Apparently this wasn't something that was done too often, at it was quite a experience.

We all secured ourselves properly in the tank. I was wondering why we all had to be so secure.

"We're going to drop in 5 minutes.." the captain said.

"Drop..??" I asked, "You mean, they're dropping us from the plane?"

"Uh, yeah.." Zastarif said, "That's what they're doing. You didn't know this??"

"I'm just a loader.." I said, "I don't know anything.. won't we uh- die??"

The all laughed and I looked around nervously, like I wanted to get out but couldn't. There was no way I could escape fast enough even if I tried. I suppose I was stuck along with the ride. As the thing started to slink forward and we dropped I closed my eyes and held on to whatever I could from the sides. I suddenly felt the ground be pulled out from underneath me and we started to fall.

I hate heights, I hate all heights. I wouldn't jump out of a plane willingly much less with a tank. Maybe it did help a bit..

"EEEE!" I screamed. "I hate this I hate this!!"

"Would you just relax? Enjoy the ride..!" someone said, I'm not too sure who I wasn't really paying that close attention. I didn't want to open my eyes until we were safe on the ground.

Suddenly I felt we were being pulled back up into the sky.. and it felt like we were almost floating.

"AH! What's happening?!" I asked, still

with my eyes closed.

"Would someone shut her up?" One voice said.

"The parachute deployed, that's what's happening. We should be safe now.."

Should be safe.. of course I wasn't aware of what was going on outside. The battlefield outside was unknown. I didn't know if we were being shot at or if we'd die as soon as we hit the ground. All my instincts were telling me "Get out, get out now!" but I had to fight it. I had to fight with all my might and it was the most unnatural state I had ever been in. I held myself back and wanted to keep calm but didn't know how to do it. I didn't want to throw up or be sick inside the tank because who'd know what they'd do then. But as soon as we landed I felt the big bang of the tank landing on the ground.

"We're here! Let's go kick some Maltaese ass!" he said, and the tank suddenly roared into life. It seemed for a moment that it was spinning in place but once it started to run it felt like we were flying again, this time on the ground. I held on tight, how the hell was I going to help in this situation? How the hell was I going to be able to do anything?

6

I didn't know, I didn't want to know what was going on outside. I just kept on loading and making sure everything was filled correctly. That's what I did I just kept going on- trying to fool myself that I was somewhere else right now and that I could get away at any time I wanted.

I could hear the bullets outside, buzzing and dinging against the tank. I could feel the rumble and chink chink chink of the treads- and the screaming outside. I just kept going and doing what was expected of me and my stomach was starting to turn. This is not what I wanted at all. I didn't want any part of this.

"Sir, we have a bogey ahead!" the Delasanto said while he looked through the view finder.

Suddenly the tank rocked a fair bit, it felt like it was hit by something.

"What the hell is that?" the captain said, "It looks like a fucking snake!"

"It missed us on purpose!! That fucker!" Zastarif screamed, as he started to fire the cannon at the enemy. The tank rocked with each blast.

"Ricochet! Zastarif you idiot! Adjust your aim!" the captain yelled, "Oritx! Get on the Vulcan cannon right now!"

"But- I can't use that thing!" I said, not wanting to move to the front.

"It's easy, point the trigger and shoot!"

I slinked through the tank, trying to ensure there was enough rounds in the cannon to reload before taking a seat behind the chain gun The weapon looked ridiculously massive to me and for a moment I wasn't sure I'd be able to turn it let alone fire the thing.

"What are you waiting for?!" The captain yelled, "Shoot!"

To my surprise the gun was extremely

easy to move. I turned and tried to figure out what I was shooting at. There was something in front of me, but it didn't look like any kind of tank I seen before. It was long, and looked round, like a snake. It seemed to be aiming it's cannon right at us, waiting.. what the hell was it waiting for?

At this time I decided it was either them or me, and I finally decided to take aim and fire this thing. The cannon started to bark and bullets poured out the side of it. The weapon was so loud and shaking so bad the whole tank rattled. I was still able to keep it on target, somehow.

"Keep firing!" The captain screamed.

The bullets flew and scattered on the other tank, the cannon fire once again and the I could swear I could see the round literally bounce right off the side. It seemed like whatever we were trying wasn't working. I could see the chips of paint flying off from the bullets, but the machine gun was starting to get hot. I could almost see it turn a glowing red as the steam started to pour off it. Then I stared for a moment. It's cannon adjusted it's aim, and it was pointing right at me.

I saw down the black eye of the cannon into this endless pit of darkness. The of that tunnel was my life and it was pointing right at me. I didn't think, I just moved- my body took over all motor skills and I ran away from the seat.

"What the hell are you doing?!" The captain said, "Get back-"

Suddenly there was a huge explosion- it was so loud all I could hear was the deaf whine of white noise from my ear drums, now damaged from the massive sound wave. Bullets started to fly all over, however, what was most troubling now was the captain was out of commission. He was knocked back so roughly his head hit the top of the tank and now he just lay limp and twitching in his seat.

"Fire! Fire!" Someone said, trying to put it out, but the cannon just kept exploding- bullets spat out every which way and I was afraid to look what was going to happen next. It felt like we were backing up but we must've hit something because we weren't moving anymore.

"Damnit you idiot! Help me!" They must've been putting out the fire, but I never looked up- I was too busy behind huddled in the corner and as far as I was concerned that must've been what saved my life.

The next thing I heard was another massive explosion- I'm not sure if the tank fired again or the Vulcan gun exploded or something- but it was much more louder and for some reason the back of the tank was suddenly on fire.

It must've been a shot from the cannon- either way the Zastarif and Delasanto were suddenly gone- where- I'm not sure. I didn't think to investigate. I looked over and saw the captain also was gone, along with his chair.. now the smell of diesel and other fluids were filling up the inside of the tank- I had to get out of here.

I wasn't sure if the other tank was still going or not, but I took and went out the emergency hatch, right into a pile of mud. It must've been an inch deep because I had one hell of a time trying to slither out from underneath it. The tanks engine was rattling and I could feel the heat coming off it.

Chapter 4

1

I tried to squirm out from under the tank, it was right next to a building and there was a small hole of the other side. Flames were starting to spit out from underneath the chassis- this was the safest route I could take. If I went out the other side, the enemy would get me for sure.

Slowly I tried to move through the gunk, I had to almost force myself to bend down lower.. my back was pressing up against the top of the metal I could feel the heat coming off my back and it was burning me instantly.

I yelled, pushed on and pulled myself

out from the corner of hole. The flames now starting to spit out. I tried to run but I slipped, I was never going to make it now.

I skidded along again, the tank now totally on fire, as I turned I could see the paint melting from over it, the words "Hope for all" now melting away like wax underneath. My eyes were blazing, hot red- I could feel they were dried out- I was seeing spots all over but I wasn't going to give in. I wasn't going to die here.

I continued to run, and at that moment I heard the whiz of something pass me by- it must've been a shot from the cannon of the other tank because I could see part of a building explode as a result. I fell over, sliding on the ground- dust and dirt now in my eyes I could barely see the alley before me. I took it and continued to run. There was no way that tank could make it through this way even with it's narrow stance.

I ran out the other side, trying desperately to catch my breath. I could feel the heat still in my lungs and coughed again, this time blood spurted out. Great.

What am I going to do now? I thought, a way, a way out- wait! I could find another tank company right?

They didn't give us any information on pick up points, what we should do if we were captured or whatever. We were expected to kill ourselves of course but I wasn't going to do that. After everything I been through so far- there was no way I was going to take that route not willingly.

I glanced around, nobody seemed to be insight, and the sounds of flames and other white noise was around. Out of the distance I could hear the rattling of that tank engine. If I didn't hurry they would surely find me here then who knows what they would do.

I decided to take a chance and continue to run the streets, I didn't even have a gun with me- they didn't give me a side arm and I didn't think I needed one- until now.

I ran across the street, up the corner and

hid behind what looked to be a cart or something. I ducked around and kept going, then hid behind what I could only guess was probably a fire hydrant of some sort.

It didn't look like anything I've seen. Nothing did. The words were all in a strange language that didn't look familiar at all. It was like I was left on another planet somewhere with no way to get out. I guess this is how it kind of ends right? Just being stuck here.. maybe it wouldn't be so bad. Maybe this place was a lot better than where I came from..but it was impossible to know.

I kept running, trying to duck and hide my way- I could hear more explosions in the distance, people yelling and screaming. I was swear it left my head but then all of a sudden I was back in the briefing room where I could hear the Colonel's voice:

"When and if our targets have been eliminated we will take care of any other civilians and soldier by using Black X."

"Black X..." I said to myself trying to

gasp for air.. I wasn't sure what it was.. but didn't they mention something about that..? Didn't they mention.. wait- Oculus, that's right. Was Black X Oculus?

I wasn't thinking right. Everything was starting to get hazy. I didn't know what was happening I was suddenly cold and didn't like it.   Here I was, in the heart of enemy territory covered with mud and listening to the weird voices in my head. There was no way I was going to get out of this alive.

2

The more I trudged along the more it seemed like I was doomed. The sky was darkening and the sounds of gunshots and explosions rang off in the distance. I know I had to find another platoon soon or else I'd be dead. At this point it didn't look like I was going to get anywhere with myself.

I wanted to sit down, I needed to go to the bathroom. I couldn't do anything else but think about sleeping. I hated this. I hated all of it. I couldn't stand the idea of being here for someone else's war or agenda. Part of me wished I would just give up.. but I knew if I did that they would not treat me kindly. I don't even know why we were "invading". Or what it was all for.

I sat down, peered down the street and I thought I saw something more. I could hear the sound of engines rumbling in the distance and it was a sound I was growing to hate. No longer did the chink of treads comfort me, it was just an indication that war and death were near.

But the thing I saw was getting bigger, at first I thought it was a wall but now.. it was that tank. That same one I saw before. Were they following me?? What was the point? I was just one person, I'm not even armed.

I got up and started to run.. I didn't wait to see what they were going to do or how they may treat prisoners. They must've seen me because the gun fired, causing a car to explode right beside me. I covered my ears, not able to take the sounds of the explosion any longer. I turned and ducked into another alley, it was empty and the smell of something rotten hung in the air. I glanced over and that's when I saw it, another soldier dead. He didn't look like one of "ours" his skin was darker, and his uniform was totally different. This must be a Maltaese..

Wait, a voice said in my head, maybe he has a gun!

I checked on him, he did indeed have a side arm.. not only that but a few feet away sat a rifle. I didn't know what kind of ammo it took. I didn't have time.. I ran out from the other side of the alley and looked around. I had to act fast- that's when I saw another tank just sitting there on the other side. It wasn't ours, but it wasn't the same tank as before. I ducked and heard voices. It seemed like they were on their break or something. I wasn't sure what they were doing but they were laughing. I had no intention in disturbing them, that's when I heard the buzzing of radio contact.

Whatever it was must've disturbed them

enough because they all got into their tank right way and left, going down the opposite way on the street.

I tried to get my barrings but I couldn't, too many strange buildings, too many weird signs that didn't make any sense to me. Everything felt futile and useless. All I could do was keep on running and hope that I didn't get into any trouble.

I waited until the tank was far enough and ran back down the same street, they must've saw me because as soon as I did the tank stopped right way, it was turning. The sound of gunshots flaying through the air- one buzzed right by my ear, I was certain if it was a few inches closer it would've hit me.

I didn't have time, I zig zagged around and ducked again, this time into another street.

"Come on, damnit! Where are you?" I asked, and something worried me. What if I was too late? What if they already all left without me?

I didn't want to take that chance. I had to

find an opportunity and seize it!

A car, I needed a car.

There were no other vehicles anywhere. The whole place seemed to be empty in cased in rumble. There was probably something functioning.

I didn't know what to do, I had to figure out something.

You aren't going to get anywhere just standing here you know, they're coming!

I knew what, stupid brain. I continued to rush and run, I was already out of breath. My heart was pounding in my chest and I could taste what felt like copper in my throat.

I hung around the corner, and bam! That's what I saw it, that's when they saw me.

It was an older man and a little girl. He wasn't in the army, they must've been trying to get away somewhere safe because he looked haggard and the little girl certainly seemed lively though frightened.

Shit! He's going to tell the others I'm around isn't he? What am I going to do?!

I held up my hands worried. I could see the little girl was only a few years older than me

"I'm not interested in fighting!" I said trying to be as clear as I could possibly be.

I backed away, they both just stared at me as if I was some kind of animal or oddity. I couldn't blame them, I kept backing away until I could run again.

I couldn't take this anymore.. I was going to have a heart attack. I stopped and panted. I was going to have to lose some weight or something. I looked around in my back pack for anything I could stand to do without.

There wasn't much, it was all necessities. Like blankets clothing, socks, lots of socks. I don't need this many socks!

I tossed them out, saw there was extra parts for weapons and tossed them too. I took the blanket out, did I need this? I growled and threw it away.

Good this is better, this is something..

I started to run again when I stopped.. I

could feel the rain coming, the drops of water on my cheeks, and what's when I heard it, the sound of voices.

3

Not just any voices, familiar voices. Voices I could understand and listen to. I could hear them laughing, I could hear them close by.

"What are you doing..?" One of the voices said. Then there was more laughter.

I rubbed my chin and gritted my teeth, trying to run towards the voices, that's when I seen what looked to be some kind of town square. I could hear shots coming. I was relieved to see colours that looked familiar, colours that seemed to be resembling my side.

I glanced up, and ducked down for a moment, curious. What they were doing?

They were laughing more and more and all I could hear was a woman screaming, and children crying. I peaked over and stared at what was going on. I couldn't believe my eyes or understand what was happening.

There were soldiers there, most of them didn't have any pants on, they were waiting it seemed, doing something to themselves like rubbing something. I didn't know I didn't see. Another was on top of what looked to be a screaming woman, he seemed to be rubbing up against her too, what was he doing?

Something was wrong here, very wrong. My instincts shot up and the urge to run now was stronger than before but I couldn't do it.

"Who's next, who's next?"

"I want her!" another voice said. It was so close for a moment I thought they were speaking to me, but I was lucky they weren't. I wanted to get out of here.

Suddenly there was more screaming and more screaming. I held my hands over my ears. They ached so much from the explosions and the yelling.

"Who are you?!" A man said looking at me, his gun was drawn. I stood up with my hands up, tears streaming down my face. He must've seen I was wearing the same uniform as he was.

"I-I-I-I-" I couldn't get any words out. Nothing worked.

"Come on!" He said, grabbing me roughly and almost dragging me out towards the others. I closed my eyes, I didn't want to see what was going on. I couldn't see, I couldn't take this anymore.

"What's this?" A voice said. It was deep and burly.

"I found this little bitch sneaking around the edge of the tank! She's wearing our uniform!"

The man looked down and stared at me, I was covered in mud. He tried to wipe away the clay stuck to my clothing and then that's when he noticed the golden star.

His eyes widened, he removed more from my name tag and that's when he realized who I was..

"You... idiot!" The Captain said. "Do you know who this is?! This is General Ortix's daughter! She is a member of the golden caste!"

I looked over at the other man who found me, the blood suddenly drew out from his face. "I'm- I'm sorry!"

The Captain frowned, he drew his gun out and pointed it to him. "Sorry isn't good enough.."

I got up and stared "No, wait! Don't kill him! Please!"

"Don't kill him? Are you sure you're a member of the Golden Caste?! I have to kill him, it's the only way!"

The other man started to run, but wasn't fast enough. He shot him in the back and he instantly fell forward. At this point the captain drew out another pistol, and glared at the man as he stood over him. It was suddenly quiet now.. so quiet I could hear myself breathing.

He held the two guns aiming for his body.

"Die you piece of shit!" He fired, I wanted to close my eyes but didn't have the time. His head exploded, skull and pieces of flesh flew all over the place. His body twitched as he lay dead on the ground.

The captained gave a glance to his body, he holstered his weapons and moved on, pointing at what was left of the other soldier.

"I want all of you to see, I want all of you to see what happens when you disrespect the Golden Circle!"

The other men didn't say anything.

"Get your fucking clothes back on we are out of here.."

"What should we do with the others?" Another soldier asked.

"Shoot them, shoot them all!"

The man nodded and grinned. He went and jumped up on to the tank while the men and children screamed, all went running. He turned and started to cut them down with the massive machine gun. It chewed up their bodies in seconds, blood splattered all over the ground and on what I could only guess was some kind of church they were pushed up against. Some did escape... But for what? To live another day? I could only guess what their lives ended up with from this point forward. Hopefully they were able to find some kind of peace in this horror that destiny had laid out for them.

4

To say I was hesitant was an understatement I was down right terrified. I didn't want to spend any time in this vehicle with any of the people I seen outside but it didn't appear as if I had a choice.

I explained to the captain what happened, and he frowned grimly.

"I seen those tanks, they're strong fuckers if you ask me. I don't think that intelligence did half as good a job as they thought they did."

"They should've told us where to go if something like this happened! I was running around like a fool all over the place and couldn't find my barrings. I was almost killed!"

"Technically you should've killed yourself once your platoon was taken out.

However, I won't fault you for that. You are but a child and a woman to a certain extent. The worse of both worlds."

I didn't comment on that. I didn't want to have an argument with the person who basically just saved my life.

"What was the point of all this..? What was so damn important that I almost had to die?" I was angry, but I didn't want to take it out on him. It wasn't his fault, but maybe he could shed some light on what the hell we were doing here in the first place.

"The point was a preemptive strike. So that we could take out Malta before they struck against us. It was a warning to ensure they wouldn't attack us.. well, the warning isn't quite given yet. We have, 1 hour to get to the extraction point. Let's pray we all get there in time before we're all doomed."

"What happens in an hour Chief?" One of the other soldiers asked.

"They will be using Black X to coat the area. Black X kills anything it touches. If we stay behind there is no hope for survival."

I started to wish this guy was my captain, at least he answered questions. Though, at this point I remembered what happened at the church. The whole bloody incident. Men, women, children, all assaulted. Nobody played any favourites, and their bodies were strung all over the steps of whatever this place of worship was. I was hoping whatever god they may worship would be kind to them in the after life, kinder than it was at the end.

5

As the tank made it's way to the rendezvous point we started to come under heavy fire. The sound of bullets pelting the metal got louder and soon and when the rain came down it was nearly hailing outside.

"Shit, this could hold back our rescue point.."

"What will happen if we don't get back there in time?" I asked.

"Well, they will either wait for us, or they won't."

A large explosion suddenly hit not too far from us, I wasn't sure if it was thunder or something else but it scarred the crap out of me. Not literally of course but it was pretty close.

"AH! Okay, we have to get out of here now!" I said.

"We're goin' as fast as we can sir! This durn thing won't go any faster!"

The captain looked through the view finder, it appeared that there was already a tank in front of us. We couldn't see any further.

"Damnit, we might have to get out and run-" The captain said.

"Are you crazy?!" Another soldier commented, "There's bullets flying all over!"

"That's jus' da rain!" The driver replied.

"Either way we can't sit here for much longer.. if they get their guns trained on us it's over-"

Another explosion came, closer, "Come on you son of a bitch!" The captain yelled. He grabbed the radio and tried to contact the tank up front. "What the hell are you guys doing! We need to make our way up there-"

"We're sorry Captain, but it looks like there has been some of kind of accident, one of the tanks up front has been hit and is on fire!"

"Goddamnit!" He said, smashing the radio to pieces. "Everyone out! We can't just sit here!"

When we got out it was pouring everywhere. It was so heavy there were sheets of white everywhere.

"Damnit! I can't see!" I said.

"We'll have to walk forward in this, come on!"

The four of us moved forward into the heavy rain, the water making my clothes harder to move in, they were getting soaked through. As we walked over we saw the other tank, still on fire. We were lucky it was raining so much now though because the firing stopped, at least from the rifles. The other heavy artillery was still trying to fire on us and get by chance.

As we continued upward, the hill seemed almost unclimbable, the mud and dirt was just collapsing.

"GAH! I can't get traction!" The other soldier said, I tried to move up but it was almost impossible, the mud was like, this strange soup of water and dirt. I managed to make up a bit of ways, but stopped before another shot hit and smashed into the side of the hill.

"Who was the idiot who thought this place up as a meeting point?!" I said into the rain, almost in reply the sky groaned and another bolt of lightning ripped across the sky.

"Come on! Go!" The captain said, Taking me and pushing me up.

I continued to climb and it got easier and easier. I was nearly at the top when the whole side started to collapse. I held on just barely as the dirt and mud collapsed on top of me, now I was totally covered. I could barely see but I was lucky the rain was around to get some of the dirt out of my eyes.

As I got up I started to hear this enormous droning sound, and this other strange noise. It was hard to describe- it sounded like something I never heard of before, like digital, robotic noise. It was like a groaning sound followed by this loud pitch beep.

I managed to get up and the captain followed after, the others were all rushing the helicopters to take us out.

I ran for the chopper, the wind and rain spilling off it doused me again in water and I was nearly clean when I reached inside the cockpit.

"What the hell is that sound?!" I asked randomly holding my hands over my ears.

"That's the bombers!! They're not waiting they're sending the bombers in now!"

What? Bombers??

"Can they even do that in this weather??"

"We're about to find out!!

The rain was slowing, and now it nearly stopped as more people came in, I was nearly crushed like a sardine can. The whole chopper wobbled as it went up into the sky for a moment I thought it wasn't going to make it, but as the rain started up again the droning noise was getting worse and worse. That's when we saw them in the distance, they looked like massive black birds, their shape was strange. Like odd birds or something, like maybe a fish. It was hard to explain how they looked, but as we took a hard turn right with the other choppers the planes started their descend. Now it suddenly sounded like they were screaming, this strange screeching noise was filling the air and I could feel the vibrations come through the chopper. It just barely made it away, we did a hard right and barely made it out from the formation. The screeching was getting louder and louder and as I looked back on them I could see it. The black smoke.

It was so thick it could block out the sun, the wind was blowing it the other way, lucky for us. Very lucky. I couldn't see any effects because the smoke was so thick.

Black X, I thought, *Oculus*.

As I turned around away from the window I was still being squished but there was no question, that was a bit closer than I wanted to be to death.

6

When we got back I was stuck in the infirmary for about a week or two. I couldn't believe how close I actually made it from death.

When I was finally released they sent me back home. It was warm on that day, the sun was illuminating everything and made the hay glow like gold.

I wanted to try to forget everything that happened, but there was no way. I still don't know what exactly went on, I didn't know but I was lucky, lucky enough.

But that isn't exactly what was on my mind, what I was thinking about more than anything was to get back to reading some of those journals I found in the basement of the old house. It had been so long since I seen it, it must've been two years I don't know. The the smell and the familiar sight of those stairs relaxed me.

And as I went down and seen the old table, covered in dust, cobwebs whisking in the wind- I saw something lay in the corner of the room, sparkling.

The glint of the metal from something I didn't see before, I didn't notice it. As I got closer I could see it was some kind of book, fairly big. Fairly familiar.

It was the Necronomicon... I thought for sure I lost it after I came back from the prison camp, but here it was, sitting on the floor.

What he hell brought it here? Brought it back..?

Could it really have been the dark man, that, Nyarlathotep maybe? Or something else... something that might have wanted me to read the book. To have it.. but why?

I still don't know for sure, but the thought was ringing back in my head. The

sound of whispering. The thought in the back of
my head that someone or something was
watching me and would continue to watch me...

I thank you for buying this, my first book. I didn't know if this was the one I was going to finish for sure. When I started it I wasn't very hopeful that this would be it, this would be the first book I would make. But now that it's over I can't help but be a little sad.

I suppose that is normal. But now as it goes, there very well might be a second book, I have more things planned for the future.

If you have any comments at all, please feel free to tweet them to me @runiestudios. Thank you very much and I hope to see you again real soon.

-May 4th 2022